MAUDLIN TOWERS

CURSE OF THE WEREWOLF BOY

MAUDLIN TOWERS

CURSE OF THE WEREWOLF BOY

CHRIS PRIESTLEY

BLOOMSBURY
CHILDREN'S BOOKS
NEW YORK LONDON OXFORD NEW DELHI SYDNEY

BLOOMSBURY CHILDREN'S BOOKS
Bloomsbury Publishing Inc., part of Bloomsbury Publishing Plc
1385 Broadway, New York, NY 10018

BLOOMSBURY, BLOOMSBURY CHILDREN'S BOOKS,
and the Diana logo are trademarks of Bloomsbury Publishing Plc

First published in Great Britain in October 2017 by Bloomsbury Publishing Plc
Published in the United States of America in July 2018
by Bloomsbury Children's Books

Bloomsbury books may be purchased for business or promotional use. For information on
bulk purchases please contact Macmillan Corporate and Premium Sales Department at
specialmarkets@macmillan.com

Library of Congress Cataloging-in-Publication Data
Names: Priestley, Chris, author, illustrator.
Title: Curse of the werewolf boy / by Chris Priestley.
Description: New York : Bloomsbury, 2018.
Summary: Maudlin Towers School students Mildew and Sponge investigate
the missing School Spoon and the appearance of two possible ghosts, one a Viking.
Identifiers: LCCN 2017050121
ISBN 978-1-68119-932-0 (hardcover) • ISBN 978-1-68119-933-7 (e-book)
Subjects: | CYAC: Boarding schools—Fiction. | Schools—Fiction. | Best friends—Fiction. |
Friendship—Fiction. | Time travel—Fiction. |Werewolves—Fiction. |
Mystery and detective stories. | Humorous stories.
Classification: LCC PZ7.P93445 Cur 2018 | DDC [Fic]—dc23
LC record available at https://lccn.loc.gov/2017050121

Book design by Andrea Kearney
Typeset by Newgen Knowledge Works Pvt. Ltd., Chennai, India
Printed and bound in the U.S.A. by Berryville Graphics Inc., Berryville, Virginia
2 4 6 8 10 9 7 5 3 1

To find out more about our authors and books visit
www.bloomsbury.com and sign up for our newsletters.

STAFF

HEADMASTER

Rev. BRIMSTONE

Mr. LUCKLESS

Mr. PARTICLE

FLINTLOCK

Miss LIVIA

Mr. STUPENDO

Miss BRONTEEN

Mr. PAINLY

PUPILS

MILDEW

SPONGE

ENDERPENNY

KENNINGWORTH

FOOTSTOOL

FURTHERMORE

HIPFLASK

FILBERT

mildew is ^ hero

MAUDLIN TOWERS
CURSE OF THE WEREWOLF BOY

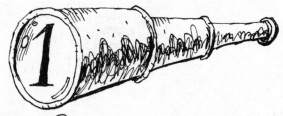

A Viking in the Ha-Ha

Mildew and his friend Sponge were taking a much needed breather on the twice-weekly jog up the side of Pig's Pike. They stood panting, gazing down at the blackened and gloom-laden, gargoyle-infested monstrosity that was their school.

Maudlin Towers School for the Not Particularly Bright Sons of the Not Especially Wealthy sat between the twin hills of Pug's Peak and Pig's Pike in the windswept north country of Cumberland, squatting like an obscenely ornate jet brooch pinned to the bosom of a sour-faced duchess.

Mildew's full name was Arthur Mildew, but no one in the school used first names. Sponge's full name was Algernon Spongely-Partwork, but everyone called him Sponge. They were not happy.

"I'm not happy, Sponge," said Mildew.

"Me neither," said Sponge with a sigh.

Mildew helped Sponge take off the backpack that their criminally insane sports teacher, Mr. Stupendo, insisted the boys wear on these runs as an extra layer of torture. Mildew groaned with the effort, dropping the backpack to the ground.

"What on earth have you got in there?" he said. "It weighs a ton."

"Stupendo caught me filling it with socks again and forced me to load it up with the contents of my trunk."

Mildew opened the pack and saw items of clothing, shoes, several books, and a brass telescope.

"Why on earth do you have a telescope?" he asked.

"I don't really know," said Sponge. "My uncle Tarquin bought it for me last Christmas. I'd forgotten I even had it, to be honest. I wish I didn't."

"Bad luck," said Mildew. "It's rather heavy."

"I know. By the way—why have you got a bandage on your arm, Mildew?" asked Sponge. "Did you have an accident over the break?"

"I've tried to tell you three times now, Sponge," said Mildew. "But every time I do, you start to hum to yourself and I get interrupt—"

"Put some pep into it, Mildew!" shouted Mr. Stupendo, stroking his horribly large mustachios, his bald head glistening like a damp egg. "Why, at your age I could lift a dead sheep over my head with barely a bead of sweat!"

Mr. Stupendo had been a circus strongman before the life of a gym teacher had tragically caught his eye.

3

"But, sir," pleaded Mildew, "my knees."

"Nonsense," said Mr. Stupendo, cuffing him round the ear and sending him sprawling headlong into the bracken. "You're far too young to have knees, Mildew. Come on! The last one to the top is a Russian."

Mr. Stupendo bounded up the path. There were pitiful groans from the boys around him as Mildew got to his feet, and their wretched, downtrodden whining suddenly stirred something in him.

"Look here," he cried, waving his fist in the air. "What say we show old Stupido what we're made of and beat the old hippo to the top?"

"Shut up, Mildew, you blister," said Kenningworth, cuffing him playfully round the ear and sending him sprawling into the bracken once again.

Mildew saw the boys disappearing up the track as he got to his feet. He spat out a piece of the indigenous flora and stared down at Maudlin Towers, a cloud-shadow darkening its already grim and grimy, gargoyle-encrusted walls. *Surely,* he thought, *this must be the very worst of schools.*

"Are you all right?" said Sponge.

"I suppose so," said Mildew with a sigh that he hoped might hint at the enormity of his despond.

"Someone needs to teach Kenningworth a lesson," said Sponge. "My mother says he—"

"Shhh," said Mildew, pointing down toward the school grounds. "Never mind Camelfroth or your mother. What's that?"

"What?" said Sponge.

"There!" said Mildew. "Running along the bottom of the ha-ha."

"The ha-ha?" said Sponge.

"Yes," said Mildew. "The ha-ha."

"The ha-ha?" said Sponge.

"Stop saying ha-ha!" said Mildew.

"But what do you mean?" said Sponge. "What are you talking about?"

"The ditch at the end of the sports field, you chump," said Mildew. "It's called a ha-ha."

"Oh," said Sponge. "Really? What's it for?"

"To stop sheep from wandering into the school grounds," said Mildew.

"Why on earth would sheep want to wander into the school?" said Sponge, shaking his head and smiling. "If I were them I'd—"

"Never mind that," said Mildew. "Look! There!"

Sponge followed Mildew's pointing finger. Running along the bottom of the ha-ha was a man. That was quite extraordinary in itself, as the only man in Maudlin Towers with any inclination to move at speed was high above him leading a chorus of "Mildew is a Russian!"

But more unusual still was the fact that this man appeared to be wearing a winged helmet and carrying, albeit with some difficulty, what looked, even from that distance, remarkably like a large ax.

"Wait," said Mildew, and after rummaging around in Sponge's backpack, he produced the telescope.

Mildew searched for the figure and focused in on its blurred form.

"There's a Viking in the ha-ha!" said Mildew.

"A Viking? But there can't be," said Sponge.

"And yet there is," said Mildew, handing him the telescope.

The boys stared at the Viking in silent amazement as he disappeared out of sight behind a laburnum bush. Before they could say anything, Mildew and Sponge were knocked down like bowling pins and trampled on by the rest of the boys as they returned from the peak of Pig's Pike.

"Last one to the bottom is a poet!" trumpeted Mr. Stupendo as he bounded by.

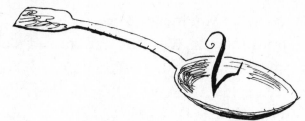

A Kerfuffle in the Corridor

Mildew and Sponge returned to the school to shower and get changed. If anything, the boys dreaded this more than the exercise itself, the freezing water for the shower coming straight from the brook that ran—rather quicker than the boys—down the side of Pug's Peak.

They dressed as hurriedly as possible and headed off to discuss the mysterious sighting, finding a quiet spot just outside the trophy room.

"Who shall we tell first about the Viking, Mildew?" said Sponge when his jaws had finally stopped rattling with the cold. "Although I wonder if they'll believe us."

"Of course they will," said Mildew. "Why wouldn't they?"

"Well, I saw it myself and I hardly believe it," said Sponge.

"I know what you mean," said Mildew. "We need to pick our moment. We don't want to be mocked."

"Any more than usual," said Sponge.

"Quite," said Mildew. "Oh no, here comes Kenningworth. Quick—in here."

The boys ducked into the trophy room as Kenningworth and some of the other boys strode down the corridor toward them. They said nothing until they heard the footfalls die away.

The trophy haul at Maudlin Towers was a sorry sight. The school had a long history of failure in almost every branch of the sporting arena. Were it not for the school's own tournaments—like the dreaded Hill-Runner's Cup—the room would be empty save for a couple of items of special significance to the school's history, like the much revered School Spoon.

"Did you hear that?" said Sponge.

"What?"

"It sounded like breathing."

"Breathing?"

"In the room with us. But not us."

Mildew and Sponge surveyed the room but saw no sign of anyone else.

"There's no one here, Sponge," said Mildew. "You're imagining things."

Sponge didn't look convinced.

"Can we go, Mildew? I don't like it."

"Of course," he said with a smile. "You are such a—"

Suddenly, there was a loud sneeze and both boys almost leaped out of their skin.

"Eeeek!" squeaked Sponge, knocking into Mildew, who banged into one of the cabinets, nearly knocking it over.

They hurried from the room without a backward glance and off to their math class with Mr. Painly, who walked to the blackboard and began to write in chalk thereon.

"Very well. If x equals 5 and y equals Brazil, what is the square root of Thursday?"

Almost two hours later, the boys staggered out of the classroom hollow-eyed and filled with self-loathing and a mind-numbing sense of limitless despair—as they did after every math lesson.

"Break time," gasped Mildew in the voice of a man released from prison after serving many years for a crime he did not commit. "At last. We have much to talk about, Sponge."

But before they could say a word, they were distracted by a great kerfuffle ahead of them.

"Look," said Sponge. "A kerfuffle."

"Yes," said Mildew. "What on earth is occurring?"

The corridor was full of boys who were being herded like reluctant rabbits toward the hall. Mildew grabbed a passing rabbit by the arm.

"Hipflask," he said. "What's happening?"

Hipflask shrugged his bony shoulders, making his hair quiver like a startled spider.

"No one knows, Mildew," he replied. "Everyone's been told to go to the hall."

"Perhaps we're not the only ones who've seen the Viking," whispered Sponge as Hipflask walked on.

"Perhaps," said Mildew.

They stepped into the river of boys and were carried along in its flow until they came to rest midway down the packed assembly hall, each boy speculating noisily with his neighbor as to what might be happening.

"Silence!" boomed Reverend Brimstone, his face glowing hellfire red, leaning over the lectern, wide-eyed, his eyebrows leaping about his forehead like crazed porcupines.

The boys were immediately quiet. Flintlock, the groundskeeper, stood silhouetted against a window, rifle in hand.

"What's he doing here?" whispered Mildew, who was sure Flintlock was looking at him.

Sponge shrugged.

"Thank you, Reverend," said the Headmaster, walking forward and smiling.

Reverend Brimstone gave one last growl before retreating, making the first couple of rows of boys step back with a whimper.

"My boys," said the Headmaster, smiling wistfully. "My dear, dear boys. As you know, I think of you as my own children. In fact, there are many of you whom, it's fair to say, I prefer to my own children."

There was a plaintive cry from the Headmaster's two sons, who attended the school. The Headmaster paid no mind, but carried on smiling benevolently.

"As you know, there was a spate of thefts at the school before we broke up for the fall holidays. A

13

baffling variety of items was stolen—Reverend Brimstone's armchair, the hall clock, and so on."

Reverend Brimstone stared boggle-eyed at the mention of his stolen armchair and lurched forward alarmingly.

"Quite what was behind these incidents," continued the Headmaster, "is hard to fathom. But we shall get to the bottom of it, mark my words.

"However," he went on, "I'm afraid—and I can hardly bring myself to give voice to the words— the theft of the hall clock pales into insignificance next to this new abomination…"

"What's gone now?" whispered Mildew with a withering look at Sponge. "The staff room doorknob?"

Sponge tittered.

"Shut up, Mildew," said Kenningworth, "accidentally" nudging him in the ear with his elbow. The Headmaster carried on.

"I'm afraid I must tell you that…" He paused and shook his head as though not quite able to believe the words he was about to utter. "Only this very morning, some boy—or boys—has—or indeed, have— stolen the School Spoon!"

The gasp that followed this revelation rattled the windows. Mildew turned to stare at Sponge.

"The sneeze, Mildew," whispered Sponge.

The Headmaster looked out at them, sadness in his eyes.

"It is hard to imagine how anyone in their right mind could even contemplate a crime of such outrageous villainy—of such depravity. I need not remind you that the School Spoon belonged to our beloved founder, Lord Marzipan Maudlin, the seventh Earl of Maudlin, whose ancestral home we are so fortunate now to inhabit.

"With no children to inherit it, Lord Maudlin, the end of his noble line, left Maudlin Towers in his will, with instructions for this glorious school to be founded within its lofty walls. The School Spoon was perhaps the greatest of all the mementos associated with Lord Maudlin, for he was given the Spoon, in person, by none other than the Duke of Wellington and King George III themselves!"

The boys gasped, as they always did when told this. Quite why the Duke of Wellington and George III had given Lord Maudlin the Spoon, or what its significance might have been to anyone concerned, was never explained.

"Someone—or ones—among you knows—or know—who is responsible for this appalling crime, and I would encourage anyone who has such information to come forward now."

There followed a long silence broken only by the damp swish of swiveling eyeballs as each boy looked at his neighbor. But no one spoke up.

"If someone were to come forward now," said the Headmaster, "then they might—and, I stress, only *might*—expect some degree of leniency. But this is your final chance."

The Headmaster looked out expectantly, but his expectation was squashed. Reverend Brimstone strode to the edge of the stage like a rabid moose.

"If you do not come forward now and are subsequently revealed to be the culprit, you will be taken to the usual place and burned at the stake!"

Some of the more imaginative boys began to sob. The Headmaster tapped the reverend's arm and whispered into his ear. The vicar looked confused and aghast.

"I've been informed that we no longer burn boys at the stake," said Reverend Brimstone mournfully. "There has apparently been a change in the school policy. Why I seem always to be the last to know, I can't fathom, but never mind. Where was I? Oh yes. Rest assured, there will be terrible consequences for all if the School Spoon is not found. Terrible!!! Parents will almost certainly be summoned!"

There was a collective shudder from the boys. There was no greater threat. Most boys would gladly be burned at the stake rather than have their parents roll up at the school at any time, kissing them and asking to be introduced to their chums— but to be *summoned by the headmaster*. It was too terrible to contemplate.

"Now I would like us all to bow our heads and think for a moment about our dear departed colleague and esteemed physics teacher, Mr. Particle, who sadly passed away during the break after a short illness…"

Mildew noticed that there was a strange glance exchanged between the Headmaster and Flintlock at the end of this request. He might have seen more had Kenningworth not knuckled him on the top of the head to encourage him to think pleasant thoughts about Mr. Particle.

"What are we going to do?" whispered Sponge afterward. He had a morbid fear of any contact with his parents.

"I don't know," said Mildew thoughtfully. "But something, be sure of that."

A Bust of Sponge

As they left the hall, Mildew and Sponge were still trying to absorb the full horror of the threat of parents being alerted when they noticed something new in the school entrance hall.

"What on earth …?" said Sponge, walking toward a marble bust of a boy that was sitting on a wooden plinth, and staring in amazement at it.

"You are showing a curious amount of fascination, Sponge," said Mildew. "You've never displayed any interest in statuary before."

"But don't you see?" said Sponge as the hallway began to quiet while boys made their way to lessons. "It's a bust of me, Mildew."

"Of you?" said Mildew. "I hardly think so. There is a heroic thrust to the jaw that—"

"But it looks exactly like me," said Sponge.

Mildew peered at the bust, then at Sponge, then at the bust.

"There is a faint resemblance, I grant you," said Mildew.

"Faint resemblance?" cried Sponge. "It's me, Mildew! Me, I tell you!"

"Calm yourself, Sponge," said Mildew. "Have you recently sat to have your bust chiseled?"

"Well, no…"

"In fact, have you ever been marbled at all?"

"Not as such…"

"Well, then."

"Lovely, isn't it?" said a voice from behind, and the Headmaster stepped beside them with the soundless approach for which he was so feared throughout the school.

"We…we…we were just admiring it, sir," said Mildew.

"We must suppose it to be a long-lost treasure of Maudlin Towers. Mr. Flintlock found it in the grounds when he was burying Mr. Particle."

"Sorry, sir?" said Sponge.

"When he was burying Mr. Particle's memorial rosebush."

"Don't you mean planting, sir?" said Mildew.

"Yes, why not?" said the Headmaster. "Off you go to class now."

He shooed them away.

"You see," said Mildew. "The bust was dug up. Who knows how long it had been there. So it can't be you, can it?"

"I suppose not," said Sponge, still sounding unconvinced.

The two boys headed off to their next class, which was history with Mr. Luckless. Mr. Luckless was one of the very few members of staff whom Mildew and Sponge did not actively fear or hate or both.

He was a short man, invariably disheveled in appearance and gentle in his manner. This combination meant that many of the boys ignored him entirely or pinged balls of paper off his balding head whenever he turned round to the blackboard to draw a map of Gaul or some such.

As usual the boys gibbered and jabbered like bored marmosets, ignoring every word Mr. Luckless uttered—or for the first few minutes at any rate.

Then Mildew and Sponge watched incredulously as, one by one, the boys began to listen.

For a curious change had taken place in Mr. Luckless. He had, against all odds and in some inexplicable way, become interesting.

Mildew and Sponge joined the other boys in listening in rapt attention as Mr. Luckless told them about the history of the land beneath their sweaty feet, taking them back to a time when the damp-stained walls of Maudlin Towers were as yet unthought of. Ancient Britons, Viking settlers, medieval peasants—all were summoned up in vivid detail.

Mr. Luckless talked with such immediacy and enthusiasm about the subject that he gave the impression he had been an actual witness to the events he was describing.

Mildew and Sponge listened intently as Mr. Luckless told them all about life in a Roman villa that he said had stood on the very same location as the school, centuries before.

The detail he went into was extraordinary, and though the brighter of the boys appreciated that there must be a great deal of invention going on, no one minded because the invention was so...so inventive.

It was almost as though the villa stood right in

front of them as Mr. Luckless described the mythical beasts pictured in the intricate mosaic on the courtyard floor and the day-to-day life of the family and servants who lived there.

Mr. Luckless seemed particularly interested in the life of the widowed owner of the villa, a Roman lady of, he assured the boys, great beauty and grace.

"Just about where you're sitting, Sponge," said Mr. Luckless, "was the well, and every day one of the servants, called Spatula, would—"

The walls were rocked by the deep and mournful toll of Big Brian, the largest and loudest of the school bells, fragments of plaster falling from the shuddering ceiling. It was a sound that none of the boys—or teachers—ever quite got used to, echoing as it did round the walls and the hillsides and leaving their insides trembling for seconds after.

"Ah," said Mr. Luckless, trying to shake the sound from his ears. "There we must leave it."

There was a wholly unprecedented groan of disappointment from the boys, and Mr. Luckless smiled, clearly enjoying this unfamiliar end to his class.

"I shall see you all yesterday," he said.

"Sir?" said one of the boys at the front.

"Sorry," he said. "I mean next year. Last week. No, no—tomorrow. *Tomorrow.*"

The boys looked at one another in mild confusion and then filed out. Mildew and Sponge wandered off toward the quad for their break.

Enderpenny's Ghost

"D o you know what I think, Sponge?" said Mildew, looking uncharacteristically thoughtful as they left Mr. Luckless's class.

"What?" said Sponge.

"Think about it. You heard old Luckless. All the Vikings from these parts have been thoroughly dead for ages."

"I suppose they have," said Sponge.

"Well, then," said Mildew.

"What?" said Sponge.

"Don't you see?"

"Not really."

"We've seen a ghost, Sponge! A ghost of one of those Vikings Luckless was burbling about."

"Goodness," said Sponge.

"And we still haven't told the others," said Mildew. "A ghost of a Viking is even better than a Viking."

"Much better," agreed Sponge. "Although you still haven't told me why you have a bandage on your arm."

"Sorry," said Mildew. "With all the excitement, I completely forgot. Well, it all began when—"

"Will there be any, you know—b-b-b—"

"Blood?"

Sponge groaned and swayed around like a dizzy weasel.

"Oh, do pull yourself together, Sponge," said Mildew.

"But you know I can't stand the sight of... I can't even say the word, Mildew."

Mildew sighed.

"Very well. Suppose instead of saying that word, I say 'soup'?"

"Soup?" said Sponge, reviving a little. "What kind?"

"It hardly matters, does it?" said Mildew. "But for the sake of it, shall we say oxtail?"

"I'm rather fond of oxtail soup."

"I know you are, Sponge, hence the suggestion."

"That's very good of you, Mildew."

"Think nothing of it, Sp—"

"Be quiet, Mildew," said Kenningworth as they passed him in the cloisters. "We're trying to hear what Enderpenny is saying."

"I'm sure it's fascinating," said Mildew sarcastically.

"Really? Then let's listen," said Sponge.

"But…oh, never mind," muttered Mildew, joining the rest of the boys clustered around Enderpenny.

"Go on, Enderpenny," said Filbert. "Tell them what you told me."

Enderpenny looked even paler than usual, and he glanced around, wide-eyed, from face to face before beginning his tale.

"Well, it all began when Footstool dared me to go up onto the roof at midnight last night."

"I never thought you'd do it, though," said Footstool.

"I can't resist a dare," said Enderpenny. "We Enderpennys are all the same that way. My father told me that—"

"But we're not allowed on the roof," said Sponge. "Or allowed out at night."

"Well, it wouldn't be much of a dare if we were, would it?" said Footstool, flaring his nostrils.

"But rule-breaking aside," said Mildew, "why are we listening to a story about Enderpenny on an ill-lit roof?"

"Because that's when I saw her," said Enderpenny.

"Who?" said Mildew.

"Whom," Furthermore corrected him.

"Shut up, Furthermore," said Kenningworth. "Go on, Enderpenny."

"I looked up and saw a light on in the attic window and crept along the roof and peered in through the glass."

"What did you see?"

"Well, the glass was awfully grimy, you understand, but nevertheless, there she was—a woman in a long white gown running around inside, wailing and throwing her arms in the air."

Sponge squealed.

"What's the matter, Sponge?" said Mildew.

"She was throwing her arms in the air," said Sponge. "How horrible."

"He's not saying the arms weren't attached, Sponge," said Mildew. "He means—"

"Oh, do pipe down, the pair of you," said Kenningworth.

"I was so surprised," continued Enderpenny, "I almost fell off the roof, and I must have made a sound because she looked up at me, staring madly."

"What did you do?"

"What do you think? I ran for it! What would you do if you saw a ghost?"

"A ghost?" cried Mildew and Sponge in unison.

"Yes," said Enderpenny. "A ghost."

"You're sure it was a woman?" said Mildew, the gears of his mind reversing back to the Viking in the ha-ha. "No sign of an ax or a winged helmet. There wasn't a beard at all?"

"No. Of course not. This was a ghostly lady."

"They have bearded ladies at the fairground," said Inkblot. "I saw one once and her beard was enormous."

bearded lady

"She was not a bearded lady," said Enderpenny. "There was no beard at all."

"There most certainly was," said Mildew.

"Oh, yes," said Sponge. "Quite definitely."

"Are you trying to say that you saw Enderpenny's ghost as well?" said Kenningworth.

"I don't see why it has become Enderpenny's Ghost," said Mildew. "Why not Mildew's Ghost?"

"Or Sponge's?" said Sponge.

"I don't think Sponge's Ghost has the right ring to it," said Mildew.

"It's called my ghost because I saw it," said Enderpenny. "Are you trying to claim you saw it too, because—"

"We didn't see your ghost," said Mildew. "We have our own ghost, don't we, Sponge? And a darn sight more interesting it was than some wailing woman. Ours had an ax and a winged helmet!"

"And a beard!" cried Sponge.

"Where did you see this so-called bearded, ax-wielding ghost of yours?" said Kenningworth.

"In the ha-ha," said Sponge.

"The ha-ha?" said Kenningworth.

"Yes," said Sponge. "It's a sort of ditch that stops—"

"I know what a ha-ha is, you nose hair," said Kenningworth. "But what would a ghost be doing there?"

31

"I don't know," said Mildew. "What was Ender-penny's ghost doing in the attic?"

"Wailing," said Enderpenny.

"There, you see," said Kenningworth. "Wailing. Everyone knows ghosts are great ones for wailing. They can't get enough of it."

"Well, Vikings don't wail, do they?" said Mildew.

"Vikings?" said Kenningworth. "What on earth are you—"

"The Viking may have been wailing quietly," said Sponge. "He was a long way away."

"A long way away?" said Kenningworth. "You never mentioned that before. How come you know all about the helmet and the beard and so on if the fellow was so far off?"

"Because we had a telescope," said Mildew.

"I might have known you'd be a stargazer, Mildew," said Kenningworth with a curl of his lip.

"I'm not interested in astronomy in the slightest," said Mildew, "and even if I was—and I'm not—we'd hardly be able to see Orion or any of his chums in broad daylight, would we?"

"Broad daylight?" said Kenningworth. "Pah!"

"What do you mean, 'Pah!'?" said Mildew.

"Well, any fool knows that ghosts are creatures of the night, Mildew."

The boys all muttered their agreement. Mildew

and Sponge exchanged glances. That did seem to have the whiff of truth about it.

"Perhaps the ghost stole the School Spoon," said Furthermore sarcastically. He was a devout skeptic and saw himself as the voice of reason.

"Which ghost?" said Sponge.

"There is only one, in my opinion," said Kenningworth.

"Or none," said Furthermore.

"How could a ghost steal anything?" said Sponge. "Wouldn't whatever it was just fall through their hands?"

"Why?" said Mildew.

"Because they're see-through, aren't they?"

"Our ghost wasn't," said Mildew.

"Well, there you go," said Kenningworth.

"Where do we go?" said Mildew.

"It wasn't a ghost at all."

"Well, was Enderpenny's ghost see-through?"

They all looked at Enderpenny.

"Now that you mention it," he said, "I'm not sure that she was. Although her white gown was not as opaque as it might have been."

There was a collective blush.

"So," said Furthermore, "it could've been an actual chap in a winged helmet and an actual lady who just happened to be wailing for reasons unknown?"

They reluctantly had to admit this was a possibility.

"But why would there be a chap in a winged helmet or a wailing lady in the school?" said Sponge.

Not one of them had an answer to this question, and after a great deal of pondering and withering looks from Furthermore, it was decided that they would investigate Enderpenny's sighting as soon as they could.

Mildew and Sponge's attempts to have *their* ghost investigated were studiously ignored—much to their annoyance—and the boys drifted off to their next class.

5

Detective Mildew

The following morning, Mildew awoke with an uncharacteristic glint in his eye.

"You have an uncharacteristic glint in your eye," said Sponge. "Are you quite well?"

"Worry not, Sponge," said Mildew. "I am filled with an indescribable hunger for adventure."

"Oh dear," said Sponge. "Perhaps it's something you ate."

Mildew picked up the well-thumbed book by his bedside and tapped Sponge's arm.

"I'm tired of being ignored, Sponge," said Mildew.

"Tired of what?" murmured Sponge, distracted by a bird flying past the window.

"Of being ignored!" said Mildew, scowling. "We must take matters into our own hands."

"But how?"

"We shall be detectives, Sponge!" exclaimed Mildew, pointing to the illustrated cover of his book. "Like the great Finlay Feathering. We shall untangle the Riddle of the Ghostly Viking and solve the Mystery of the School Spoon!"

Finlay Feathering was the hero of a series of detective stories by Henry H. Henry, and Mildew was a devoted reader. *The Peculiar Goings-on at Gravely Grange* was a particular favorite and Mildew had read it several times. In it, Finlay Feathering solves a similarly despicable theft—that of Sir Rupert Gravely's ruby toe-ring.

"But we don't know how," said Sponge. "We have no experience at detectivating."

"Everything we need to know is in here," said Mildew, tapping the book. "All we have to do is ask ourselves, 'What would Finlay Feathering do?'"

"And what will we reply?" asked Sponge eagerly.

"Well, it depends on the circumstances," said Mildew.

"Gosh," said Sponge admiringly. "You are clever, Mildew."

"True," said Mildew. "But it's very clever of you to see it, Sponge. So many don't."

"You hide it so well, Mildew."

Mildew frowned.

"Let's start with the School Spoon. We shall be heroes if we solve that, Sponge. Imagine."

Sponge tried but could not.

"The first thing Finlay Feathering always does is he decides who the suspects are."

"And who are the suspects?" said Sponge. "In this case, I mean?"

Mildew put his hand on his hip and stared off into the middle distance detectively.

"Well, everyone, I suppose," said Mildew. "Even ourselves, if we are to be thorough. We were in the trophy room, after all."

"But I didn't do it," said Sponge defensively.

"I'm afraid we can't just take your word for it, Sponge," said Mildew. "After all, that is precisely what the actual culprit would say. We have to go where the evidence takes us."

"And where does the evidence take us?"

"Nowhere at the moment," said Mildew. "We

don't really have any. Evidence, that is. Apart from the absence of the School Spoon."

"And the ghosts," said Sponge.

"The ghosts may be red herrings," said Mildew.

"Ghostly red herrings?"

"Precisely."

"But might the ghosts be involved in some way?"

"I don't think ghosts burgle, Sponge," said Mildew. "They are more ones for scaring the bejabers out of folk, and that sort of caper. I don't think they are much interested in spoons of whatever value."

"It seems an odd coincidence though, doesn't it?" said Sponge. "That the School Spoon should go missing and two ghosts appear."

"If indeed they were ghosts," said Mildew.

"Or herrings," said Sponge.

"Not herrings," said Mildew. "Red herrings."

"Aren't red herrings herrings?"

"Not necessarily," said Mildew. "They could be a pair of slippers or a vicar."

"A vicar?"

"Yes. Or a hairbrush. A red herring can be anything. Whereas a herring is restricted to being a fish. And not just any fish, Sponge. Only a herring. Does that help?"

"Not really."

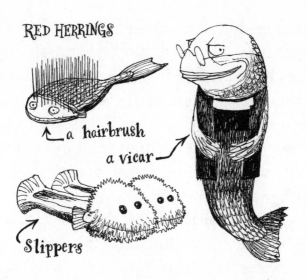

RED HERRINGS

a hairbrush

a vicar

slippers

Sponge's brain had begun to ache terribly.

"A red herring is a phrase we detectives use to mean something that distracts us from solving the crime. Something that seems relevant at first but turns out not to be. Like algebra."

Sponge shook his head.

"It's frightfully difficult, isn't it—this detectivating business."

"Detecting," Mildew corrected him with a look of great seriousness on his face. "That's why it requires the keenest of minds, Sponge. We must look at each suspect in turn and eliminate them from our inquiries."

"But there are so many," said Sponge. "Where will we start?"

Mildew stroked his chin as he'd noticed Finlay

Feathering did at times like this and stared off meaningfully into the distance once again.

"We must begin with the teachers," said Mildew. "There are fewer of them, and so it will be quicker to eliminate them."

"And which of the teachers shall we start with?"

"Why, with the Headmaster, of course."

Sponge gasped in shock.

"You surely cannot think that the Headmaster could be guilty of stealing the School Spoon?"

"Everyone is under suspicion," said Mildew, leaning toward Sponge and peering at him. "Everyone…"

Sponge whimpered. Mildew stood up.

"We shall begin this very day!" he said. "Come, Sponge, to the Headmaster's office!"

Charcoal Gray

M ildew and Sponge walked round the
cloistered quadrangle of Maudlin
Towers as rain began to fall from a
charcoal gray sky.

"What will we be looking for?" said Sponge.

"We are looking for any strange behavior," said
Mildew.

Sponge raised a quizzical eyebrow. Mildew took
his meaning.

"Stranger than normal," Mildew emphasized.
"The culprit always gives himself away to Finlay
Feathering eventually. All we need to do is observe."

They both peered observantly at the door to the
Headmaster's office, edging closer.

"Can I help you, boys?" said a voice behind
them.

They both turned with a small shriek of alarm to find the Headmaster looming over them, an indulgent smile on his face, his hands clasped together.

"What brings you two boys inside on such a glorious day?"

Mildew and Sponge looked toward a nearby window where hail hammered into the glass like shotgun pellets.

"We…we…we…," burbled Sponge.

"Yes?" said the Headmaster, leaning closer.

"We are writing a piece for the school newspaper, sir," interrupted Mildew.

The uppermost points of the Headmaster's smile began to quiver.

"Not about the theft of the School Spoon, I hope."

"No, no, sir," Mildew reassured him. "We are doing a piece about the life of the school."

"The life of the school, eh?" said the Headmaster, his smile returning to its full width. "That sounds marvelous. And you have time to do that and rehearse for the play?"

"The play?" said Mildew.

The Headmaster winked and tapped his nose.

"Of course," he said with a chuckle. "Not a word!"

Mildew and Sponge exchanged a puzzled glance.

"I must say, it's gratifying," continued the Headmaster, "to find you boys taking an active interest in the school for a change. What will the piece consist of exactly?"

"Well, sir," said Mildew, wondering what such a thing might entail. "I—that is, we—thought that it might—possibly—be a good idea simply to spy on—to *observe*—the goings-on of the teachers— I mean the school—in all its detail."

The Headmaster nodded approvingly.

"Splendid! I can hardly wait to read it. You won't forget to mention Mrs. Leecham, will you? She gets frightfully upset if she thinks her nursing endeavors are being overlooked or undervalued."

"Rest assured, sir," said Mildew. "The school nurse is one of our prime suspects—I mean *subjects*."

"Excellent," said the Headmaster. "Then I suppose I'd better let you carry on with your observing."

"Thank you, sir," said Sponge.

"Whom exactly are you observing at this present moment in time?"

"Well, sir," said Mildew. "Actually, it's you, sir."

"Me?" said the Headmaster with a broad grin. "Well, how wonderful. What do you want me to do?"

"I suppose you really ought to go about your business," said Mildew. "As if we weren't here."

"I see," said the Headmaster. "How intriguing."

The Headmaster stood self-consciously for a moment before nodding and wandering away.

The boys paused for a few seconds before heading after him.

At a safe distance, the boys observed the Headmaster as he strolled around the school and grounds, amiably chatting to all he encountered and handing out words of encouragement to staff and students alike.

The hideous weather did not in any way dampen his spirits, although it did dampen Mildew's notebook and make it increasingly difficult to write on.

And so the boys were very happy when the Headmaster returned to the confines of the school. They followed him as he walked around the ancient cloisters, his hands behind his back.

"Headmaster, sir," said the school secretary, scurrying up beside him. "Bad news, I'm afraid. The caretaker says the boiler will need replacing. It will be very expensive, he says."

"Oh dear," said the Headmaster. "It can't be helped, I suppose."

"And the beams in the dining hall are infested with worms, sir."

"Are they?" said the Headmaster with a wry smile. "Little devils. Anything else?"

"There appears to be a small fire in the east wing, Headmaster."

"Would you be so good as to send someone to put it out, when they have a moment?"

"Yes, Headmaster."

"Excellent."

None of this seemed in any way to erode the Headmaster's mood. He bowed to two passing fresh-faced boys from the lower school—but then came to a sudden halt.

"I say," he called to the boys amiably. "If you could be so good as to come back here for just a moment."

The boys turned, ashen-faced, and edged back toward the Headmaster, whose black-gowned figure drifted toward them like spilled ink.

"I hate to impose on you, but might I make a small inquiry?" he asked, smiling down at the boys.

"S-s-sir?" said the larger of the two small students.

"I was wondering," he said, pointing a long finger at the other boy's socks, "whether my eyes were deceiving me in this poor light. Are those socks you are wearing black, by any chance?"

"Yes, sir," said the boy. "But I—"

"Splendid," said the Headmaster, his teeth now glinting horribly. "Then my eyes are not as impaired as I had feared. That certainly is a relief, is it not?"

"Yes, sir," said the boy, backing away a little. "But—"

"One gets to my age and one fears the loss of one's faculties, so it is heartening to know that my eyesight at least is still functioning."

"Yes, sir," said the boy. "But—"

"All would be absolutely perfect, indeed, were it not for the fact that the school regulations of Maudlin Towers specifically demand that the socks of the boys of the lower school must be of no color other than charcoal gray."

"Yes, sir," said the boy. "But—"

"And are these socks charcoal gray?" said the Headmaster, leaning ever nearer to the trembling boy, his smile now a trifle crocodilian.

"N-n-no, sir," admitted the unfortunate child.

"Are you an anarchist, perhaps?"

"No, sir."

"Might I see you tomorrow in a kilt or a toga?" he said, addressing the two boys.

"No, sir," they both replied.

"Then would you both be so good as to pop along and explain yourselves to Reverend Brimstone?"

"But, sir," said the larger of the boys, "my socks are charcoal gray."

The Headmaster smiled horribly at the unfortunate lad until, with the other boy, he scampered away, blubbering, in the direction of Reverend Brimstone's office.

"Ah, boys," said the Headmaster, noticing Mildew and Sponge peering round the corner. "How are your observations going? Are you managing to capture the flavor of things?"

"I think so," said Mildew. "I think so, sir."

"Excellent," said the Headmaster.

And with a smile and pat of both boys' heads, he went on his way, humming a few bars of Bach.

"Perfectly normal," said Sponge.

"Agreed," said Mildew, crossing the Headmaster's name from his list.

7

A List of Suspects

Mildew and Sponge used the physics lesson they would have been having with the as yet unreplaced Mr. Particle to wander the school observing the teachers going about their respective duties.

The first classroom they came to was that of Miss Bronteen, the English teacher. She was reading a sample of poetry by one of her pupils, a boy called Farnsworth. When she had finished, she stood at the window, gazing wistfully out onto the moors— as she always did.

"I feel o'ertaken by a sudden melancholy, Farnsworth," she said, without turning round. "As though my very soul were sinking into the abyss. What sad and awful fate has forced me to bear witness to your cruel attempts at verse.

"Have I ever told you about the time...?"

"I feel o'ertaken by a sudden melancholy..."

"Gloom. That's the key to painting, boy..."

"Bof"

"Begin, Gosling..."

You will write 'I am a dull and worthless fellow' one thousand times."

Mildew and Sponge moved on. The next classroom was Mr. Drumlin's, the geography teacher, a big and brash Scotsman much given to interminable tales of his days as an explorer.

"Have I ever told you about the time I was attacked by the Sticky People of the Lower Kushti with nothing to defend myself but my own trousers and a rolled-up copy of *The Illustrated London News*?"

"Yes," came a weak voice from the back.

Mildew sighed, and the boys carried on along the corridor until they came to a class being taught by Miss Bleu, the French teacher, who sat with half-closed eyes, flaring her nostrils.

"Miss?" said a hapless boy at the front of the class. "Are we going to get our homework back?"

There followed a pause of between twenty and twenty-five minutes before Miss Bleu gave a heavy shrug, pouted, and said, "*Bof*," before slouching back into her usual state of ennui.

The math classroom was next, presided over by Mr. Painly.

"It is my privilege," he said, wild-eyed, "to initiate you into the mystical world of numbers, into the magic of the ancients, the sacred realm of the

Kabbalah. But we shall start with the four times table. Begin, Gosling…"

Mildew and Sponge peered through the window of the door to the art room to see their art teacher, Mr. Riddell, flailing his arms about and clutching at his hair.

"What are you doing, Lamprey? How many times have I told you to stop using so many colors? Colors give the viewer indigestion of the optic senses. If the good Lord had wanted color, he would never have invented England. Color is for Spaniards, Hawkins. Gloom. That's the key to painting, boy. Gloom!"

Mildew and Sponge observed the behavior of all the teaching staff, together with Miss Pernickety, the school secretary; Mr. Scurry, the caretaker; Miss Foxing, the librarian; Mrs. Glump, the school cook—even the dreaded Mrs. Leecham, the nurse—and all displayed their usual catalog of eccentricities. Flintlock, the groundskeeper, was the last one they observed.

"I know you," he growled at Mildew.

"Well, I am here every day," said Mildew nervously.

Flintlock walked over and stared at Mildew.

"You're that one that…"

Flintlock cast a quick glance at Sponge and shook his head.

"Never mind. But I've got my eye on you. Anyway, be off; I've got work to do."

Mildew and Sponge needed no further encouragement to leave.

"Whatever did he mean?" asked Sponge.

"I have not the slightest idea."

The boys looked at each other resignedly.

"They all seem to be behaving perfectly normally," said Mildew.

"Yes," agreed Sponge. "They are as deranged and peculiar as they usually are, but no more so."

Mildew nodded. They both saw Kenningworth and a group of boys ahead, but did not steer another course in time.

"Seen any more Vikings, Mildew?" said Kenningworth with a grin.

There was a ripple of chuckles.

"Scoff away," said Mildew. "Sponge and I have more important matters to attend to."

"Ha!" said Kenningworth.

"More important than anything you're doing, I bet," said Sponge.

"Well, you won't be interested to hear that some of us are going ghost-hunting in the attic tonight, then," said Enderpenny.

"G-g-ghost-hunting?" said Sponge.

"But it's a secret," said Kenningworth. "So no blabbing, you two."

"Are you trying to say we are the sort who blab? I'll have you know that—"

"They've gone, Mildew."

Sure enough, the boys had moved away, Kenningworth's braying voice fading into the distance.

"I wonder if our culprit may be among the boys," said Mildew with a frown.

"We cannot observe all the boys in the school, Mildew," said Sponge. "We'll be old men by the time we've finished."

"You're right, of course," said Mildew. "We shall have to decide who among them is more likely to have committed the crime."

"Well, first on my list of bad sorts would be Kenningworth," said Sponge. "He is an absolute blot."

Mildew smiled and sighed.

"Ah, Sponge," he said. "The first lesson of any detective mystery is that the crime is never done by the likely suspect."

"It isn't?"

Mildew shook his head.

"The more a person seems likely to commit a crime, the more it rules them out," said Mildew. "I'm afraid Kenningworth is simply too obviously odious to be guilty."

"You're sure?"

"Quite sure," said Mildew.

They decided to draw up a list of other likely culprits among the boys.

"But not too likely," said Mildew.

"So we are to make a list of unlikely suspects?"

"In a manner of speaking," said Mildew.

Sponge shook his head in bewilderment and the boys walked on.

"Mildew?" said Sponge a little later.

"Yes, old twig?"

"You don't think Mr. Luckless might have been behaving oddly, do you?"

"How so?" said Mildew.

"With his strange familiarity with the Roman villa that he says was once here and with his sudden lack of boringness. And then there's all that business with getting the time of the class confused."

Mildew chuckled and placed a hand on his friend's shoulder.

"Oh, Sponge," he said. "Well done for trying, but I can't see old Luckless as a thief, can you?"

"I suppose not…But then what reason would anyone have for stealing the School Spoon?" said Sponge. "It's a spoon. There's hardly a spoon shortage."

"Good point, Sponge," said Mildew. "But you mustn't say 'reason.'"

"I mustn't?"

"No," said Mildew. "Finlay Feathering calls the reason for doing something dastardly 'a motive.'"

"A motive?"

"Exactly."

"Why doesn't Finlay Feathering just say 'reason' like the rest of us?"

"Because detectives aren't the rest of us, Sponge, that's why."

Sponge nodded thoughtfully.

"So what re—motive might someone have for stealing the School Spoon?" said Sponge. "It can't really be that valuable. Outside of the school, I mean."

"I don't know," said Mildew. "It's true that to the casual observer the School Spoon does appear to be rather like any other spoon, and a thief would surely be more likely to steal the School Diamond in the cabinet next to it."

Sponge nodded. That did seem odd, come to think of it. The School Diamond was rather large.

"Sometimes," said Mildew, "when Finlay Feathering has an especially tricky case, he goes and talks to his very clever uncle, Sir Farley Feathering."

"Excellent," said Sponge. "Where does he live?"

"He lives in London," said Mildew. "In Berkeley Square to be precise."

Sponge frowned, disappointed.

"Oh. That's a long way away. I can't see how we—"

"And, well, he is fictional, Sponge."

"Ah. That makes him seem even farther away."

Mildew shook his head.

"We will have to find our own clever older person," said Mildew.

"Do you yourself have a clever uncle, perhaps?" said Sponge.

"No," said Mildew. "I have two uncles, both of whom are as dull as a Wednesday afternoon and as dim as chickens."

"Then who?" said Sponge. "As you know, I am entirely uncle-less. Unless you count my aunt Bernard."

"No, Sponge," said Mildew. "I think we will have to find someone closer to home than your aunt Bernard. Come on. I have an idea…"

Mr. Luckless Is Consulted

Mildew had decided they would tell Mr. Luckless about the ghost they had seen in the ha-ha and find out if he had any thoughts on the subject.

Being the history teacher, he seemed the obvious first choice for anything to do with the past. It took them a while, but eventually they found him starting up the stairs toward the attic.

"Sir," said Mildew. "Sponge and I were wondering…"

"Yes, my boy," he said, looking at his watch with a nervous twitch about the eyebrow region. "I am most frightfully busy."

"You know you were telling us all about the goings-on that took place in the hereabouts of Maudlin Towers in days of yore."

"Hereabouts…days of yore, yes…" said Luckless, nodding distractedly and glancing up the stairs.

"Well, sir," said Mildew. "What would you say if we told you that we'd seen a ghost, sir. From those very same days of yore."

"A ghost, eh?" he said, tweaking the end of his mustache. "I'm afraid I don't really have time for a ghost story. Perhaps another ti—"

"No, sir," said Sponge. "This isn't a ghost *story*. This was an actual ghost. Although there seems to be some concern about the un-see-through-ness."

"The un-see-through-ness?"

"Yes—you know, sir—how ghosts are always described as see-through? Well, ours wasn't. See-through. Do you see?"

"Well, what did this ghostly chap look like to make you think he was a ghost?" said Mr. Luckless with a forced smile, casting another furtive glance up the stairs. "Headless knight, was he? Clanking chains, perhaps?"

Here Mr. Luckless waved his arms around and made a *woo-woo* noise that Mildew found very irritating.

"No, sir," he said, frowning. "It was the fact that he was a Viking, and what with you telling us about the goings-on in bygone days—of all the history that went on hereabouts—you said there was a Viking village here, sir, do you remember?"

"Well, yes…" said Mr. Luckless, staring off a little nervously in the direction of the sports field. "But what makes you so sure it was a Viking? Or a ghost for that matter? Might you have been mistaken?"

"Well, he certainly looked like a Viking," said Mildew. "He had a winged helmet, a beard, and a big ax. And he had to be a ghost, didn't he, because there could hardly be a real Viking loose at the school, could there? I mean, how could he get here? It's not as though he could travel through time, is it?"

Mr. Luckless began to shake.

"No, quite…" he said, looking away again. "Travel through time? Ha! The idea!"

Mr. Luckless seemed to return to the chaotic Luckless of old, dropping the papers he was carrying.

"Is everything all right, sir?" said Mildew.

"What?" said Mr. Luckless, gathering his papers and books. "Of course everything's all right, Mildew. Ghosts! Vikings! Pah! What nonsense."

"That's what Furthermore said about Enderpenny's ghost," said Sponge.

"There's more than one?" said Mr. Luckless, a nervous tic now taking hold of his right eyebrow.

"He says he saw the ghost of a woman, sir. In a long white dress and waving and wailing."

Again, Luckless staggered sideways and stared at the boys, whimpering.

"The ghost of a woman, you say?"

"Yes, sir?"

Mr. Luckless gazed off toward the attic.

"Was she as beautiful as a summer's dawn?"

Mildew and Sponge looked at each other.

"Er…he never said, sir," said Mildew. "Are you quite all right, sir? You look ill."

"I'm quite all right, thank you," said Mr. Luckless unconvincingly.

"If you want my opinion," said Mildew, "End-erpenny is having us all on, or he ate some bad cheese or something."

"Anyway, a group of the boys is going to the attic tonight to try and find this so-called ghost of his," blurted Sponge.

"Shhh!" hissed Mildew.

"What?" said Mr. Luckless. "But they can't. They mustn't."

"I did try to say we weren't allowed out at night, sir," said Sponge. "But they wouldn't listen."

"But...but...but," butted Mr. Luckless.

"What were you thinking, Sponge?" said Mildew.

"It just came out," said Sponge.

"I'm afraid I can't allow it," said Mr. Luckless. "I will...I will have to inform the Headmaster."

"You can't let on you know, sir," said Mildew. "The boys will think we've blabbed."

"We have blabbed," said Sponge.

"*You* have blabbed. There's no we," said Mildew, as he turned to Mr. Luckless beseechingly. "Sir, you can't snitch on us. After all, you don't want to lose the goodwill of the boys so soon after winning them over..."

Mr. Luckless's eyes had been darting back and forth like confused sardines, but he now seemed to come to his senses.

"Of course not," he said. "You're quite right, Mildew. I shan't say a word. You have my word on it. On not saying a word, that is."

"Thank you, sir."

"What time is this jaunt to take place, may I ask?" said Mr. Luckless.

"Midnight, sir. That is, after all, the traditional hour for this kind of thing."

Mr. Luckless nodded and wandered off, muttering to himself.

Ghost-Hunting

The boys waited until the school was quite quiet and then, as one, they emerged from their beds and padded off in the direction of the dormitory door.

Ordinarily, Mildew and Sponge would not have rushed to be part of such a caper, but Mildew felt that, as a detective, he needed to be on the scene. Besides—Mildew was irked at the notion that Kenningworth was so ready to give credence to Enderpenny's tale whilst being so dismissive of their Viking. He wanted to be there when Enderpenny's ghost was debunked.

In fact, in his enthusiasm, Mildew had seen to it that not only were he and Sponge to join in the search of the attic, they had volunteered to be first out of the dorm to check if the coast was clear.

So it was that, shortly before midnight, Mildew and Sponge acknowledged the solemn nods of their fellows and Mildew slowly opened the door with a high-pitched whine.

"Stop whining, Mildew," hissed Kenningworth. "Someone will hear."

Mildew and Sponge slipped through the door, closing it quietly behind them, to stand in the gloom of the landing. All was quiet and still.

"It's very quiet," whimpered Sponge.

"That's a good thing," whispered Mildew. "After all, if there was a ghost we'd hear—"

"We'd hear what?" said Sponge.

But Mildew pointed to the stairs leading up to the attic. Sponge heard it too now. There was the distinct and unpleasant sound of footsteps and breathless gasps and groans heading their way.

The two boys bravely tried to claw their way back into the dorm, but the boys inside had clearly heard the noise too and seemed willing to sacrifice Mildew and Sponge for the greater good.

Terrified, Mildew and Sponge turned to see a figure looming toward them—a figure that turned out to be Mr. Luckless staggering down the stairs with a rolled-up carpet in his arms.

"Ah!" he cried. "Is it that time already? She refused to cooperate."

"Who did?"

"What? It. I meant *it*. The carpet. The carpet refused to be rolled up. You know how some carpets are."

"But you said 'she,' sir," said Sponge.

"Did I?" said Mr. Luckless. "Well...that's because I've had too much coffee."

"Coffee, sir?" said Mildew.

"Yes, absolutely," said Mr. Luckless, gasping and straining under the weight. "I'm afraid it drives me loopy. That's why I've got this carpet, you see. It's the sort of mad nonsense I get up to when I've had too many."

"You roll up carpets and carry them away, sir?" said Mildew.

"I do," gasped Mr. Luckless. "It's appalling, I know, but there we have it. Never drink coffee, boys, that's my advice."

Mr. Luckless grimaced and took a couple of steps back, almost falling over with the strain.

"Would you like to put the carpet down, sir?" asked Sponge kindly.

"No," said Mr. Luckless. "Thank you. Best not. She might escape. *It* might escape. It might—you know—roll off and escape. The way carpets do."

"You didn't happen to see any ghosts while you were in the attic, did you, sir?" asked Mildew.

"Ghosts?" said Mr. Luckless. "I don't think so."

Mr. Luckless was sweating now and turning redder by the second.

"Of course," he said. "You were to go looking for your ghostly wailing woman tonight. I'd completely forgotten. I'm not getting in your way, am I?"

"Only a little bit, sir," said Sponge.

"Well, then, I really must be getting on," he said. "I'll leave you to it, if you don't mind."

"Of course, sir," said Mildew.

"Good hunting," said Mr. Luckless over his shoulder. "And don't worry. Shan't say a word."

Mr. Luckless staggered away down the stairs, making a variety of noises, some of which sounded a little like those a squashed woman might make.

Mildew and Sponge waited until Mr. Luckless had disappeared entirely before knocking on the dormitory door.

"Open up, you bounders," said Mildew.

After a pause, the door creaked open and the boys peered out.

"Fine sorts you are," said Mildew, "leaving us out here. Supposing it had been a ghost."

"Well, we were hardly going to let the ghost into the dorm," said Enderpenny. "Be reasonable, Mildew."

"Be reasonable?" cried Mildew. "Be reasonable? That's easy for you to say, safe on the other side of that door."

"Except we weren't really, were we?" said Furthermore.

"What are you burbling about now?" said Kenningworth.

"Ghosts are supposed to be able to walk through walls, aren't they? I hardly think a door would hold them back."

The boys gasped and stared at one another while Furthermore shook his head despairingly.

"What was old Luckless doing here?" asked Kenningworth. "You didn't blab about what we were planning tonight, did you, Mildew?"

"Blab?" said Mildew. "Of course not. The very idea!"

"The very idea?" said Kenningworth. "You are a famous blabber, Mildew."

"Me? A blabber?"

"Yes!" said Kenningworth. "You're just the sort who blabs."

"No, he isn't," said Sponge.

"Thank you, Sponge," said Mildew.

"Then what was he up to?"

"He was making off with a carpet from the attic," said Mildew. "He seems to have lost his marbles, if you ask me."

"A bit of a coincidence he should choose to do that the very night we are to hunt for the ghost," said Furthermore.

"I suppose," said Mildew. "But that's the thing about coincidences, isn't it?"

"What is?"

"Erm...I've lost my thread," said Mildew. "Sponge—you explain."

"What? Why? How?" spluttered Sponge.

"Oh, for goodness' sake," said Furthermore. "Let's go and find this 'ghost,' shall we?"

There was a collective gulp, and after a moment they headed slowly toward the stairs. For all his skepticism, Furthermore seemed no keener than anyone else to be the first to the attic door. Suddenly, the building was shaken by a dozen mighty clangs from Big Brian, high above them. It was midnight!

Once the dust had settled, it was Kenningworth who finally plucked up the courage to open the attic door, and they all tried to get through at once, not wanting to be left behind any more than they wanted to be in the attic. Sponge was the first through, popping like a cork into the darkness.

At first the boys could see nothing at all, but after a few moments their eyes adjusted to the gloom, and the little bit of light coming in through the skylights from the moon above afforded them a view of the contents of the long attic room.

It was basically a storeroom for everything that was not in daily use, and clearly there were items that must have been there since the days when the Maudlin family still inhabited Maudlin Towers.

There were pieces of furniture, old packing crates and boxes, a large suit of armor, mirrors, paintings, more carpets and rugs, but, to everyone's relief, no sign of a ghost.

"Look at this," said Sponge to Mildew.

Sponge pointed to a plate and cutlery on a table. Remains of food were visible on the plate.

"Was old Luckless having a midnight feast up here?" said Mildew.

"Perhaps he was building his strength up for carrying the carpet," suggested Sponge.

"And look at this bed," said Mildew. "It looks as though it has been slept in."

"So it does," said Sponge. "He did look tired."

"But that's because he was carrying a massive carpet, Sponge," said Mildew. "One doesn't get tired before one exerts oneself, does one?"

"I do sometimes," said Sponge. "The thought of it, you know."

"Something fishy is afoot here," said Mildew.

But the boys were already heading out of the attic and Mildew and Sponge, filled with a sudden dread of being shut in that place alone, ghost or no ghost, headed after them.

A New Latin Teacher

Mildew and Sponge did not enjoy Latin, and so they were not especially upset that their lessons would be curtailed by the death of Mr. Particle, who had taught Latin as well as physics. Hopes of a Latin-free day were dashed, however, when Mr. Luckless appeared before them.

"Attention, boys," said Mr. Luckless, coughing and straightening his tie. "I have great pleasure in introducing your new Latin teacher."

At first they all assumed Mr. Luckless was talking about himself, but to their astonishment a tall and rather beautiful woman walked into the classroom. As Mildew stared, openmouthed, the sound of harp music filled his ears.

"Beeswax!" shouted Mr. Luckless. "How many

times have I told you? Practice your harp in the music room and in your own time!"

Beeswax put his harp down with a series of discordant twangs.

"Boys," continued Mr. Luckless. "This is Miss Lovelier—I mean Livia—Miss Livia. Please give her a warm Maudlin Towers welcome."

An arrhythmic clatter of handclaps followed, with a few more twangs from Beeswax's harp. Mr. Luckless left, walking into the doorframe in his efforts to have one last look at Miss Livia. Miss Livia looked at the boys nervously before breaking into a broad grin.

"Ah, Spudge!" she said, on seeing Sponge. While Sponge spluttered with confusion, Miss Livia strode forward, lifted him from his chair, and hugged him tightly, showering him with kisses.

The boys were aghast, and none more aghaster than Mildew, who stared at his friend in shock and disbelief.

Miss Livia's English was not as fluent as her Latin. She had a very strong foreign accent. But she was such a delightful and attractive Latin-monger—and such an improvement on Particle—that the boys sat in rapt attention. Even Mildew was eventually mesmerized by her smiles, her wild gesticulations.

When the lesson ended, the boys left, little wiser than before about the mysteries of the Latin language, but both of them were grinning like ninnies at the recollection of some passing glance Miss Livia may have given them.

"Sponge?" said Mildew when they were alone. "What on earth was that all about? How do you know this Miss Livia and why is she so free with her affections?"

"I have no idea!" said Sponge.

"Come now, Sponge," said Mildew. "She knew your name."

"No, she didn't," said Sponge. "She called me Spudge."

"Close enough, don't you think?" said Mildew.

"I swear, Mildew," said Sponge. "It must be a case of mistaken identity. I have never seen that woman before in my life."

"Strange you should say that," said Enderpenny as he walked past. "Because she looked oddly familiar somehow. It's been bothering me ever since she walked into the classroom."

"Familiar?" said Mildew. "How? She's new to the school."

"I know," said Enderpenny. "Even so…"

"Perhaps she is a relative," suggested Sponge. "An aunt, perhaps."

"No," said Enderpenny. "I have twelve aunts, but she isn't one of them."

"Twelve aunts?" said Mildew with a shudder.

"I'm afraid so," said Enderpenny. "Many of them affectionate."

Mildew shook his head gravely.

"I have it!" cried Enderpenny. "But how? I mean, what on earth…?"

"Yes," agreed Mildew. "What on earth are you on about, Enderpenny?"

"Well, don't you see?"

"Not entirely," said Sponge.

"She's none other than the ghost in the attic!"

"What nonsense is this, Enderpenny?" said Mildew. "She isn't a ghost. She almost squeezed the daylights out of poor Sponge there."

"But that's it," said Enderpenny. "I just thought she was a ghost because of all the wailing and the white dress and it being nighttime and such. But it must have been Miss Livia in the attic."

"But why would she be in the attic?" said Sponge.

"I don't know, old chum," said Enderpenny. "But it's her, I swear."

Enderpenny walked on, leaving Mildew and Sponge to mull.

"Do you remember the plate and so on?" said Sponge.

"Yes," said Mildew. "And the bed. Why would a ghost need food? Good Lord—Enderpenny's right this time. I think Miss Livia must have been up there secretly and Mr. Luckless knew all about it! It must have been her inside that carpet. That's why he was almost twanging his spine with the weight."

"Why would Mr. Luckless be keeping a beautiful woman locked in the attic, Mildew? It makes no sense."

"I don't know, Sponge," said Mildew. "Teachers are strange creatures. But I have a feeling it has something to do with the theft of the School Spoon!"

"How so?"

"Merely a hunch, Sponge. That's something that detectives have from time to time."

Sponge frowned and opened his mouth to speak but was cut off before he could.

"I believe that, for whatever reason, Mr. Luckless and this Miss Livia person—if indeed that is her name—may be in cahoots."

"In cahoots?"

"Yes. What if they planned the robbery together? Beauty and coffee have clearly driven Luckless insane. I think they are intending to escape with their hoard."

"I'd hardly call the School Spoon, a chair, and an old clock a hoard, Mildew."

"I think they have only just begun, Sponge," said Mildew. "Soon the School Diamond and the contents of our trunks will be gone too."

"No!"

"I believe so," said Mildew.

"But I thought you said old Luckless couldn't possibly be a thief," said Sponge.

"I think you'll find it was you who said that, Sponge."

"Was it?"

"I think so, yes. In fact, I'm almost certain."

"What a fool I was."

"Don't be too hard on yourself, Sponge. Luckless and this so-called 'Miss Livia' may well be teacher criminals. But they've met their match this time!"

"Hurrah!" said Sponge.

Mildew peered at him. "I'm afraid you are still under suspicion, Sponge," he said.

"What?" said Sponge. "How? Why?"

"We still haven't gotten to the bottom of why Miss Livia was so effusive in her affections toward you."

"But there is no bottom to be gotten to, Mildew," said Sponge. "I have never seen that woman before in my entire life!"

"Very well," said Mildew doubtfully. "But I will still have to keep you under observation."

"If you think that's necessary."

"I'm afraid I do."

The Temporo-Trans-Navigational-Vehicular Engine

Mildew and Sponge found a quiet spot in the cloisters to plan their next move. Mildew explained that it was traditional for a detective to confront the criminal and accuse him, or indeed her, of his or her crime face-to-face.

"But isn't that frightfully dangerous?" asked Sponge.

Mildew nodded.

"Yes," he replied. "But we detectives laugh in the face of danger, Sponge."

"We do?"

Sponge felt that they might be more of the whimpering-in-the-face-of-danger types but he was eager not to let Mildew down, so he followed him to Mr. Luckless's classroom, where they found their history teacher musing.

"Sir," said Mildew. "We're sorry to interrupt your musing, but I'm afraid the game is up."

"The game?" said Mr. Luckless. "Whatever can you mean?"

"We know about Miss Livia and the attic."

"What? Who? Where? How? What? Who? How?"

"There is no need to gibber, sir," said Mildew. "We saw you creeping down the stairs, remember? The night we looked for Enderpenny's so-called ghost."

"But what has that to do with Miss Loveyou— I mean Livia?"

"I believe the carpet you were carrying contained Miss Livia, sir," said Mildew. "That you and she are scheming together and that she is posing as a preposterously fetching Latin teacher."

"All right, all right," said Mr. Luckless. "You have forced it out of me! I confess!"

"You stole the School Spoon!" cried Mildew and Sponge in unison.

"What?" said Mr. Luckless. "No, of course I didn't."

"Then what are you confessing to, sir?" said Mildew.

"To traveling back in time!" said Mr. Luckless. "To being bewitched!"

And with that, he collapsed into pitiful sobbing.

Mildew and Sponge looked on, equally baffled.

"What do you mean, sir?" said Sponge, not wanting to dwell on the bewitched part of the confession. "Traveling back in time?"

"Just that," said Mr. Luckless. "I have journeyed into the past."

"Have you been drinking coffee again, sir?" asked Sponge.

"No—I swear!" said Mr. Luckless.

"But no one can travel in time. That's impossible. Isn't it?" said Mildew.

"A few weeks ago I'd have agreed with you, Mildew," said Mr. Luckless. "And some days I wish it was a dream from which I will awake. But I need to tell someone, and as my most loyal, if not my brightest, pupils, it might as well be you."

Mr. Luckless asked the boys to take a seat, which they did. It was a moment or two before Mr. Luckless was able to continue.

"It touches on the death of poor Mr. Particle," said Mr. Luckless. "You were shocked to hear of his demise, I'm sure."

"Of course, sir," said Mildew. "Although I did owe him homework, so..."

"He was a very private person, but we forged a friendship," said Mr. Luckless, frowning at Mildew. "When I went to collect his belongings from his room, I discovered a small wooden box with an accompanying letter addressed to me and telling me to open it in the event of his death. And so I did."

"And what was in the box, sir?" asked Sponge.

"A large key and a note in Mr. Particle's spidery handwriting. The note read—"

"The bothy?" said Sponge.

"Yes," said Mr. Luckless. "It's that small hut at the far end of the sports field. You may not even have noticed it."

Neither of the boys had noticed it. The sports field was a place of great emotional trauma for both of them, and they committed little of what went on there or thereabouts to memory.

"I had, of course, not the slightest inkling of what the 'everything' I would find there might be. I had known that he had a little workshop he took himself off to when the school day ended, but neither I, nor any of the other staff, had ever received an invitation to enter it.

"I naturally assumed the place would turn out to be full of books and scholarly studies, and there were indeed many items of that kind. But nothing could have prepared me for the sight of the curious machine in the center of the room."

"Machine, sir?" said Mildew. "What kind of machine?"

Mr. Luckless grabbed both boys by their arms and pulled them close with a sudden violence, staring into their eyes with a wild intensity.

"A machine for traveling through time!" he cried. "I call it a temporo-trans-navigational-vehicular-engine."

"Not 'time machine?'" suggested Sponge.

Mr. Luckless stared at him for a moment.

"Well, I suppose one could call it that…"

"Could we see it, sir?" said Sponge.

"Yes," said Mr. Luckless after a moment's thought. "It is a marvel—an incredible marvel—but it has also become a terrible burden. I'm a simple man, boys—it has all become too much. It feels better to share it with you. Mr. Particle was the only member of staff I could confide in. But you must agree to absolute secrecy."

"Of course, sir," said Mildew.

Mildew and Sponge accompanied Mr. Luckless through the school and out across the sports field to where, sure enough, there was a small, dilapidated bothy.

The boys entered the building after their teacher and could see straight away where several of the recently stolen school items had ended up.

The machine was essentially a high-backed leather armchair—the Reverend Brimstone's chair, in fact—but underneath the chair, and attached to it at the sides, were all manner of cogs and levers and dials. Largest among these dials was the instantly recognizable face of the hall clock.

"So it was Mr. Particle who stole all the school stuff!" said Mildew. "Who'd have thought it."

"I think 'stole' is perhaps unfair. 'Utilized without permission' would be more accurate."

"So it was Mr. Particle who utilized the School Spoon!" cried Mildew and Sponge in unison.

"The School Spoon?" said Mr. Luckless. "I'm afraid Mr. Particle had passed away before the theft of the School Spoon. He is not your thief. And neither is Livia, before you start."

Mildew and Sponge sighed. The mystery seemed to be getting deeper rather than shallower.

"A machine that travels through time," said Sponge, wide-eyed, turning back to the chair. "How amazing! Where would you go, Mildew?"

"Oooh," said Mildew, putting a fist on either hip and jutting out his jaw. "What about London when Sir Francis Drake and all those Elizabethan chaps were about?"

"Or Egypt when the pharaohs were in charge?"

"Or the Battle of Hastings," said Mildew. "From a safe distance."

"Or—"

"I'm sorry to disappoint you, boys," said Mr. Luckless. "But the temporo-trans-nav…the time machine…only travels through time. It can't travel in space. Mr. Particle was very specific about that."

"Can't travel in space?" said Mildew. "What do you mean, sir?"

"I mean that it can only travel along the timeline of this actual place—of the school. Nowhere else."

Mildew and Sponge looked at the machine, then each other, then the machine again. What had seemed utterly amazing only minutes before now seemed not quite so utterly amazing.

"But what's the point of that, sir?" said Mildew. "This is the dullest place in the world and probably always has been."

"It is true that it has been very dull for quite a long time. Leaving aside loopy Lord Maudlin a century ago, Maudlin Towers and its environs was pretty dull until one gets back to medieval times, but every time I arrived there they seemed to have the plague or some such and so I decided to go back further still…"

"Wait!" said Sponge. "You've been back to Roman times, haven't you, sir?"

Mr. Luckless nodded and put his hand over his mouth, stifling a giggle.

"I have!" he said. "I really have!"

"That's why your lessons stopped being so…" Mildew stopped, unable to finish the sentence.

"Boring," said Mr. Luckless. "It's quite all right. I know it's true. I was a boring teacher. I was awful.

But now I have you in the palm of my hands. Oh— you don't know what it's like, boys."

Mildew peered at the machine, craning to see behind.

"But how is it powered, sir?" said Mildew. "I can't see a steam engine of any kind."

"Well, Mr. Particle explained that it is powered by bursts of energy in the brain when the brain is befuddled and stressed."

"So it's powered by confusion?" said Sponge.

"I suppose it is," said Mr. Luckless. "In a manner of speaking."

"How did you know how to work it, sir?"

"The details are here," said Mr. Luckless. "In this book."

He pointed to a small leather-bound notebook hanging by a length of string from the arm of the chair.

"And that Roman lady," said Sponge, "the one you told us about in class—that's Miss Livia, isn't it?"

Mr. Luckless nodded.

"But how on earth did she come to be here, sir?" said Mildew.

"I brought her back. I am in love with her!" declared Mr. Luckless. "There! I've said it!"

Mildew and Sponge exchanged a glance, not entirely sure how they were supposed to respond and wishing Mr. Luckless had chosen someone else to declare this to.

"Then I wonder, perhaps," said Mildew after a moment, eager to change the subject, "if you might not have also brought a Viking back with you."

"I can't have. I haven't been back to Viking times, only Roman," said Mr. Luckless. "You can see the device. I would know if there was a Viking with me."

"But then how did Miss Livia travel back—er, forward—with you, sir?" said Sponge. "There only appears to be room for one."

"She…that is…she…*ahem*…sat on my lap."

Both boys blushed and Mildew struggled, without complete success, to stop himself from smirking.

"Smirk away, Mildew," said Mr. Luckless, frowning. "I am not ashamed. My love for Livia is a fine thing, a pure thing, a noble thing."

"But to bring her back to the school, sir," said Mildew.

"I know. I had said my farewells, but just as I was about to leave, Livia leaped onto my lap and, well, here we are. Now that she is here, I haven't had the heart to send her back. I had asked her to be quiet in the attic, but she's very hot-blooded, you know."

Mildew shook his head. Why grown men made such fools of themselves over the female of the species he would never understand.

"But, sir," said Mildew, "you can't keep a Roman lady in the school."

"We aren't even allowed pets," said Sponge. "So it would hardly be fair."

"No," he agreed. "You're right, of course. But Livia is very much her own woman. She wants to be here. She is not my prisoner. It's all a frightful mess. What am I to do? What am I to do?"

Here, Mr. Luckless gave himself up to terrible sobbing.

"What am I to do?" he wailed.

Mildew and Sponge looked at each other awkwardly and Mildew placed a hand on Mr. Luckless's shoulder as he had seen his mother do when his father was sobbing terribly.

"There, there, sir," he said. "It can't be as bad as all that."

94

But privately, Mildew thought that it probably was as bad as all that and quite possibly worse. Mr. Luckless took out a handkerchief and bassooned into it. He slowly returned to a state of relative calm, straightening his collar and mustache.

"But, sir," said Sponge, "it's only a matter of time before someone realizes she isn't a Latin teacher at all, but a Roman lady. Enderpenny has already recognized her as his ghost."

"Merciful heavens!" said Mr. Luckless. "She must go back, I know. But she's being very difficult. She refuses to let me take her back to her own time. She's very forceful."

"But she can't want to spend her days in Maudlin Towers. Who in their right mind would—"

"I may have promised to take her to Rome."

"Rome?" said Mildew.

"I may have done that. In a weaker moment. And she was very keen on that idea. Very keen. She's very hard to say no to."

"Was she not happy in Roman Cumberland?" asked Sponge.

"She wasn't enjoying Britannia at all, I'm afraid. Especially not this particular damp and drafty bit of it."

"Who can blame her?" said Mildew.

"But won't Rome be a tad different nowadays?" said Sponge.

Mr. Luckless put his hand to his forehead and nodded.

"I have tried to explain that to her," said Mr. Luckless. "But she refuses to accept what I'm saying. My Latin is not quite up to the task and her English…"

"It must be very confusing for her," said Sponge.

"I'm certainly confused," said Mildew.

"I think we all are, Mildew," said Mr. Luckless.

The three of them stood, pondering their communal confusion.

"I shall try and get her to accept that she needs to go back," said Mr. Luckless, attempting to apply some firmness to the set of his jaw. "Although things will seem very dull without her."

"My mother always says there's a lot to be said for dullness," said Mildew.

Mr. Luckless nodded sagely.

"She may be right, Mildew. She may be right."

Christmas Is Canceled

"I t feels very satisfying to have solved our very first mystery," said Sponge as they walked to assembly the following day.

"But we haven't, have we?" said Mildew. "We've solved the Mystery of Enderpenny's Ghost, but we weren't really trying to solve that one. And to be fair, Enderpenny was on the way to solving that himself. We are no nearer to solving the mystery of the School Spoon, are we, Sponge?"

"I suppose not," said Sponge. "When you put it like that."

"We haven't even solved the mystery of the Viking in the ha-ha."

"No," agreed Sponge. "We aren't very good detectives, are we?"

"Don't be too hard on yourself, Sponge," whispered Mildew as they took their places.

Reverend Brimstone was in a particularly enthusiastic mood.

"...and your sin-stained souls will be the playthings of cruelly imaginative demons for all eternity. Ye shall be toasted like marshmallows before the everlasting bonfires of hell..."

And so on and so on. Eventually Reverend Brimstone simply ran out of breath and collapsed, like a deflated balloon, into a nearby chair.

"Thank you, padre," said the Headmaster with a smile. "A lot to think about there as always..."

The Headmaster looked at the assembled boys.

"It is with great regret that I have to inform you that no one has come forward either to confess or with information that might lead to the restoration of the School Spoon, and no one has been discovered to be the thief.

"It has been suggested to me that my threat to inform parents was too severe and so I have decided that I will not carry this out..."

There was a mighty cheer from the assembled boys.

"I have instead decided that there will be no Christmas holiday this year. You will all remain at Maudlin Towers for the duration."

There was a gasp. Not just from the boys, either. The staff knew that they would be forced to stay as well, and they looked forward to escaping the dank hallways of Maudlin Towers as much as any of the boys. The hall emptied in dismal silence.

"Mildew," said Sponge afterward, his lips quivering like jellied eels, "I simply have to have a Christmas holiday. It's all that keeps me going."

Mildew nodded.

"I always go to my aunt Bernard's," said Sponge. "She's the only Spongely-Partwork to really understand Christmas. She dresses up as Santa and paints her beard white. We always have a lovely time. I shall not survive the rest of the year without it, Mildew."

Mildew sighed. Even his own dour and mirthless parents relaxed their grim routine for Christmas, and Mildew shared Sponge's dread of doing without.

Like all the pupils at Maudlin Towers, he had heard terrible tales of boys whose parents had left them at the school for Christmas and the gloomy and joyless holiday they had been forced to endure.

Mildew saw an opportunity for him and Sponge to be heroes and was determined to grasp it. They simply had to discover the thief and free the boys—and, more importantly, themselves—from this terrible fate.

"But I don't understand," said Furthermore as he passed by. "Why did the Headmaster not summon our parents?"

"Hmm," said Mildew. "You have a point there. That is odd."

"Very," said Furthermore. "It's almost as though he didn't want parents snooping about the place for some reason. Maybe he doesn't want them to find out about the ghosts."

Furthermore chuckled to himself and wandered off.

"If only we could see who had taken the Spoon," said Sponge.

"Indeed," said Mildew.

"We need one of those fortune-teller people," said Sponge.

"What good would that do?" said Mildew. "That would only be useful if the theft hadn't happened. They see into the future. But it's already taken place."

"Yes," said Sponge. "If only we had some way of seeing into the past."

The two boys stared at each other wide-eyed.

"Of course! The time machine!" said Sponge.

"There's only one thing to do!" declared Mildew. "Someone must go back in time to just before the theft took place and foil the criminal."

"That's very brave of you, Mildew," said Sponge.

"Of me?" said Mildew. "I was thinking more that someone of your small stature would travel quicker."

"Oh, I'm sure that's not how it works," said Sponge. "And if it did, then probably a taller person would be better suited."

"How's that?" said Mildew.

"The extra weight would stop the machine wobbling about."

"You imagine that the time machine wobbles about in time?"

"It might. You don't know."

Mildew had to admit that he didn't.

"We could both go," said Sponge.

"Both?" said Mildew. "There's no room."

"I could sit on your lap," said Sponge.

"You will most definitely not sit on my lap," said Mildew. "Just because Luckless's Roman lady sat on his lap doesn't mean the world has gone mad. I shall pretend you never said that."

"I apologize unreservedly, Mildew," said Sponge.

"Accepted," said Mildew.

Sponge studied his shoelaces for a moment or two.

"But it doesn't matter about laps or whatnot," said he. "Because neither of us knows how to use the machine."

Mildew waved this argument away as though it were a sleepy wasp.

"Pish," he pished. "How hard can it be? Old Luckless figured it out and he's not exactly the sharpest splinter in the toe, is he?"

"True," said Sponge. "That is very true."

"Come on, Sponge," said Mildew. "There's no time to lose. Sooner or later Luckless will finally take his Roman girlfriend home, and then who knows whether he will return. This may be our only chance to use the time machine."

Mildew and Sponge sneaked past the Headmaster's office and out the front door and edged along the side of the building until they reached the corner and could see the bothy across the sports field.

"We need to move at a greater speed than normal, Sponge," said Mildew. "Are you up to the task?"

"I think so," said Sponge, steeling himself.

The two boys set off at a brisk lope, and it was almost a minute before they stopped, doubled up and gasping.

"I can't…go…on," gasped Sponge. "Leave me. I shall stay here and die alone."

"Nonsense, Sponge…old…friend," gasped Mildew. "We shall…die…together…"

"You boys!" yelled a voice like an elephant exploding in a tunnel.

Mildew and Sponge turned to see Mr. Stupendo marching toward them.

"What are you doing on the lower sports field before noon?"

Mildew and Sponge searched each other's faces for clues as to how they might answer and found nothing of any practical use.

"Well?" bellowed Mr. Stupendo.

"We were going for a run," said Sponge, surprising himself almost as much as Mildew.

"A run?" said Stupendo. "You?"

"Yes, sir," said Sponge. "We…we…we…have been wanting to get fitter, sir."

"Really?" said Mr. Stupendo. "And why would that be?"

"Yes," said Mildew. "Why was that again, Sponge?"

"Because…because…because we have decided to enter the annual Hill-Running Tournament, sir."

Mr. Stupendo stared at Sponge for some considerable time and then, putting his hands on his hips, burst into frighteningly enthusiastic laughter.

"Well, that's excellent news," he said, when he had calmed himself. "I'll put your names on the list right now. On with your training, boys. You'll need it! Whoever comes last has to run it again from the start!"

Mr. Stupendo strolled away toward the school. Mildew glared at Sponge. And then, after a good amount of time, glared at him some more.

"The Hill-Running Tournament, Sponge?" he said.

"I panicked," said Sponge.

"What are we going to do?" said Mildew. "I shan't survive an ordeal like that. My knees…"

"Me neither," said Sponge. "I get dizzy running downhill."

"When have you ever run downhill?"

"I'm not sure," said Sponge. "But I can imagine it. Vividly. And it's horrid."

Sponge staggered about dizzily. Mildew groaned like a wounded walrus.

"Let's not think about it just now," said Sponge eventually. "Let's stick to our plan. We'll worry about old Stupido at a later date."

Mildew nodded.

"Very well," he said. "But if it's all the same to you, I think we should forgo the running and proceed at a swift amble."

"Agreed," said Sponge.

And so the boys arrived at the bothy and the time machine, finding everything as it had last been.

"Right," said Mildew. "Let's see how this thing works."

Both boys flicked through the book and stared at the time machine with what each hoped might suggest serious deliberation. Several minutes later, there they remained.

"It looks frightfully difficult," said Sponge.

"Chin up," said Mildew. "Come on, let's just prod the time machine and see what happens."

"Do you think that's wise?" said Sponge, wiping his nose.

"The British Empire was founded on people who had the courage to prod things without worrying about the consequences, Sponge. Come on. We must be brave."

Mildew sat in the chair and peered at the workings on either side of him.

"You see here, Sponge?" he said, looking at the diagrams in the book and then at the selection of clock faces to his right. "I think these must signify the time. Look—there are a couple of places marked. They're in different handwriting. One must be Luckless's and the other Particle's."

"But it all seems very confusing," said Sponge.

"It's powered by confusion," said Mildew, moving the hands of the clock to the time noted in the book. "Don't you remember? It ought to go like a dream. I'll meet you in the library when I'm finished. Wish me—"

"I wonder what this lever does," said Sponge, pulling on said lever.

There was a bright flash and a whine like a small dog with a cold falling down a well, and Mildew blinked once or twice, momentarily blinded, and found that Sponge and the bothy had disappeared and were now replaced by a large group of rather grumpy

folk, who, a cursory glance led Mildew to suppose, were, in all probability, Vikings. The machine must have taken Mildew back to one of the places Particle had recorded in the book. So he was the Viking connection, not Luckless.

"Greetings," said Mildew, standing up. "I come in peace."

The crowd growled. Mildew flinched.

"I'm a friend of Mr. Particle's," said Mildew.

There was much murmuring at this pronouncement. They clearly knew who Particle was, but as they grabbed Mildew and led him away, he didn't get the impression that they liked him very much.

Mildew Deserts Himself in His Hour of Need

M ildew was unceremoniously frog-
marched through the village, complaining all the while that there must be
some terrible mistake.

"Excuse me!" he protested. "Could I possibly go
back to my time machine? I'd love to stay but my
friend will be wondering where I am."

If his hosts understood him, they did not feel
the need to respond. The crowd grew in number
as others came out of their wooden houses to see
what the commotion was. A boy about his own age
seemed to have a fascination with Mildew's clothes,
grabbing at them as he passed. He was particularly
taken with the school badge on the breast pocket.

"Hey!" shouted Mildew as the boy pawed at him
again. "Hands off my blazer."

The boy scowled and stuck out his tongue. Eventually they arrived at a very tall and curiously carved post, with various symbols and patterns cut into its length and a vicious-looking animal skull at the top. The entire crowd of villagers, man, woman, and child, bowed reverentially toward the post.

Mildew was baffled as to the significance of the object, but it was clearly very important. While he stood there pondering, he was suddenly dragged toward it and tied up with thick cords.

Having secured him to the post, the crowd stood back and bowed their heads again, as though in prayer. Mildew was just about to speak when every one of the assembled crowd threw back their heads and howled like wolves.

Just then a man leaped forward, his head covered in a wolf skin, so that the head, complete with jaws and teeth, was worn like a hood and the rest of the skin like a cape. He jumped and snarled in a frenzy.

It was a startling sight and sound and Mildew tried not to panic but didn't quite succeed, whimpering and straining against his bonds. The crowd moved away and began to prepare some sort of celebratory feast from which he, it seemed, was to be excluded.

"Untie me, you brutes!" he cried.

But no one seemed very interested. Especially a rather muscle-bound character who was studiously sharpening a double-headed ax. Every now and again he would look at Mildew and then sharpen the ax a little more, chuckling to himself.

Mildew had the distinct feeling that his situation, already some way from ideal, was about to get very much worse. Particularly when the man holding the ax looked up and pointed at him, then at the ax, and then ran his finger across his throat before chuckling in time to his sharpening.

Mildew closed his eyes in the vain hope that this might all turn out to be a dream. But when he opened them, he was still tied to the post and the Viking was still sharpening his ax. Mildew began to whimper softly as night closed in.

Sacrifice! That was the only explanation. For reasons unknown, these Vikings had decided that Mildew would make a fine sacrifice. They seemed to have a bit of a thing about wolves. Was Mildew to be sacrificed to their wolf god?

A large bonfire was lit and a great feast was laid out. It appeared that his execution was going to be a lively event. Mildew was pained by thoughts of all he might have achieved had he been allowed to live. He couldn't be sure that he would have achieved anything especially wonderful, but that was hardly the point. Lots of people didn't do anything especially wonderful and didn't get sacrificed to wolf gods. It wasn't fair.

Then Mildew noticed something moving in the shadows beside a group of wooden buildings ahead of him. *What new horror is this?* he thought, as the thing began to move toward him in the gloom.

He was about to cry out when the bonfire light revealed the thing to be none other than Mildew himself, saying, "Shhh."

"I've come from the future to save myself!" whispered Mildew with relief. "How resourceful of me."

Without responding, the other Mildew reached into the bound Mildew's jacket pocket, fumbled around for a moment, and then left.

"Wait!" cried Mildew.

But the other Mildew disappeared into the night.

"I've deserted myself in my hour of need," said Mildew miserably.

Suddenly the clouds parted and a bright full moon shone down on the scene before him, and the light from it glinted on something in front of Mildew. Somebody was walking toward him carrying a knife. Mildew gasped and fell into a faint—although he couldn't fall far, because he was tied to the post.

Moments later, Mildew felt himself coming round briefly, aware of a snarling sound that was so close it might have been in his own head. His body shook violently as though he was having a fit. Just as he was opening his eyes, his head was struck by a sudden pain, and he fell into unconsciousness once more. As he drifted off, he had the strongest sensation that Sponge was nearby, and even fancied he saw his friend standing some way off, looking concerned.

"Dear Sponge," he murmured, mid-slump.

When Mildew came to next, he found himself in an untidy heap beside the pole, his bonds cut through, his clothes shredded. There was a terrible odor, the major part of it bringing to mind the heady whiff of large damp dog.

Perhaps I'm dead, thought Mildew, quickly checking that his head was where he had last left it. It was, but Mildew wondered if heads were restored in the afterlife.

He was toying with the notion that he might be in heaven, when a procession of Viking villagers made its way gingerly toward him.

I don't understand, thought Mildew. *What has happened to me?*

The villagers encircled him, and Mildew whimpered, fearing that in this vulnerable semi-clad state, he would be once more at the mercy of the ax. Things always seemed worse, semi-clad.

"Please don't kill me again," said Mildew. "Or if you haven't killed me, don't kill me at all."

But very quickly it became clear that the villagers meant no harm. Far from it. They were now, for whatever reason, afraid and in awe of Mildew, and their chief bowed to him and offered some clothes to restore his modesty.

Though the clothes they offered him smelled of old weasels, Mildew was only too happy to accept. But the villagers felt that Mildew had to be appeased further and so gifts were brought forward.

What's going on? thought Mildew. *First they want to lop my noggin off, then they behave like I'm a god or some such.*

Alarmingly, the very ax that had been intended for Mildew's execution was brought forth, but the chief handed it solemnly over to him, and Mildew accepted it with equal solemnity (and relief), until the weight of it nearly pulled his arms from their sockets.

"Thank you," gasped Mildew. "This is awfully decent of you."

The chief looked at his people and they at him, seemingly unsure as to whether they had done enough. Mildew couldn't help looking at the chief's rather fine winged helmet.

Following Mildew's gaze, the bystanders started pointing and shouting. The chief shouted back angrily, but the villagers pointed at Mildew and shouted some more. The chief muttered and grumbled, but eventually took off his helmet. To Mildew's surprise, his beard was part of the helmet and underneath the Viking was clean-shaven.

The chief placed the helmet solemnly—albeit with some reluctance—on Mildew's head, tickly beard and all. Unfortunately it was far too large, even with Mildew's mop of hair, and sank down over his face so that he could see nothing at all.

There was some concern among the villagers at this turn of events, until someone went to fetch a large bread bun from the aftermath of the feast. The chief removed the helmet and placed the bun inside before returning it to Mildew's head. This seemed to do the trick, and Mildew smiled and thanked the chief warmly, causing him to sigh with relief, and the whole village cheered.

The newly helmeted Mildew was hoisted onto the chief's shoulders and paraded about the village before being returned to the time machine, where he was ceremoniously deposited. Mildew had the distinct impression they were eager to get rid of him.

Unfortunately, Mildew had no more idea how to work the time machine now than he'd had back in his own time, and though the village hovered over him expectantly, he was at a loss to understand how to set the controls.

The chief seemed to sense Mildew's confusion and helpfully pointed to the clock dial.

"Yes, yes," said Mildew. "But how do I set it to get me back to Maudlin Towers?"

Mildew surprised himself at this desire to return to Maudlin Towers—it was a desire he had never thought himself capable of.

He decided that desperate times called for desperate measures. There was nothing else for it. He was going to have to try to use his brain.

Mildew stared at the clock faces. He could see that Mr. Particle had marked where the dials corresponded to the times he had visited, but that did not help him in knowing where the dial should be set for return.

He tried to think how the clock had looked when he had first examined it, and he remembered thinking that it was odd because there was no minute hand.

Ah-ha! thought Mildew. I *thought there was only one hand because both hands were at twelve. So perhaps if I move the minute hand back to twelve …*

Mildew moved the hand backward to twelve and gripped the end of the lever.

"Goodbye, Mr. Viking, sir—and thanks for the ax."

With that, Mildew pulled the lever. There was a bright flash and whine and he was back at the bothy.

"I did it!" cried Mildew. "Wait till Sponge hears about my adventures."

Mildew Eats Some Very Old Bread

M ildew peered out the doorway, wondering how long had elapsed since his trip to the Viking age. There didn't seem to be anyone about, which meant he was probably supposed to be in class and would be missed. Given the way he was dressed, he thought he ought perhaps to conceal himself by skirting round the sports field using the ha-ha.

Mildew sneaked along the edge of the bothy and clambered down the slippery grass bank of the ha-ha, before moving along its length with as much stealth as he could in a heavy winged helmet, carrying an ax.

It was only when he was halfway along, and about to turn the corner that would lead to the school, that it occurred to him to look up at Pug's

Peak, where he saw the distinctive silhouette of Mr. Stupendo and a group of boys thundering down the hillside. And there, a little ways below them, stood two boys, one of them holding to his eye something that glinted in the morning light.

Good Lord! thought Mildew, stroking his Viking beard. *Of course! I'm the ghost in the ha-ha!*

He moved on and hid behind a bush, watching his other self and Sponge head off after Stupendo and Kenningworth and the others.

This must mean that I have returned to an earlier present than the present I left, as I'd hoped, thought Mildew, boggling his mind as he did so. *Perhaps I'm getting the hang of this time-traveling business.*

Mildew thought that the best thing to do would be to get changed out of his Viking things and into his school uniform. He climbed out of the ha-ha and headed off toward the school. Entering by the east door, he peered each way down the corridors. There was no one about.

Mildew took one step and a hand was placed on his shoulder. He turned to see the Headmaster looking down at him.

"Ah, Mildew," the Headmaster said, his smile already beginning to fade alarmingly as he surveyed Mildew's attire. "Do you have any explanation for your wilful disregard for the school uniform? I'm sure you do."

"I'm…I'm … I'm…"

"Yes?"

"I'm rehearsing for a play, sir," said Mildew.

"A play?" said the Headmaster, peering at Mildew suspiciously. "I haven't been told about any theatrical performance."

"It's a surprise, sir," said Mildew.

"A surprise?"

"Yes, sir," said Mildew. "None of the masters know, sir. It's something we boys have written ourselves. They'll be very cross that I've let the cat out of the bag."

"How lovely!" said the Headmaster, his good humor returning. "No need to worry. I shan't let on that I know anything about it."

He tapped the side of his nose and winked.

"Thank you, sir," said Mildew.

"And when is this performance?" said the Headmaster.

"I'm afraid I've said too much already," said Mildew.

"Ah," said the Headmaster, tapping the side of his nose again. "Understood. May I?"

The Headmaster took the ax from Mildew's hands and swished it through the air, almost taking Mildew's head off with the second swish and achieving what the ax's Viking owner had failed to do.

"Marvelous what they can do with some cardboard, glue, and a spot of paint," said the Headmaster. "The magic of the theater, eh, Mildew?"

"If that's all, sir?" said Mildew, taking back possession of the ax.

"Of course, of course," said the Headmaster, beaming. "Run along."

Mildew managed to get to his dorm and change clothes, stowing the ax and helmet in his trunk at the end of his bed.

I'm famished, he thought. *Time travel and being in fear of one's life does wonders for the appetite.*

Luckily he remembered the bread roll the Viking chief had put inside the helmet and he ate a few mouthfuls to keep him going. Mildew nodded approvingly. Considering it was several centuries old, it wasn't half bad.

Mildew Pockets the Spoon

Mildew was about to head back to the time machine when he had a sudden thought. Having come back in the time machine to an earlier time than when he'd set off, he now realized he might be in a position to catch the School Spoon thief red-handed. After all, the Spoon had been there when he and Sponge had popped into the trophy room to discuss the Viking in the ha-ha. The Spoon must have been stolen shortly afterward.

If he could hide himself in the trophy room, Mildew might catch a glimpse of the culprit, or even apprehend him (if he was one of the smaller, weaker boys). The Christmas holidays would not be canceled, and although no one but Sponge would know, Mildew would have saved the day.

Giddy with the excitement of these thoughts, Mildew scurried with uncharacteristic purposefulness and speed toward the school trophy room.

The School Spoon was still safely in its cabinet. Mr. Stupendo's class—including him and Sponge—would only just now be returning from their run. Mildew decided he would hide behind one of the cabinets and wait to see who came in.

He was surprised at how exhausting doing nothing and just waiting turned out to be. He yawned and blinked and yawned. He tried desperately to think unsleepy thoughts, but it was all to no avail—within moments he fell into a deep snooze, woken only by the noise of whispered chatter nearby.

Mildew peered out from behind the cabinet and was astonished at the strangeness of seeing himself and Sponge standing beside the School Spoon.

"There's no one here, Sponge," said the other Mildew. "You're imagining things."

Sponge didn't look convinced.

"Can we go, Mildew? I don't like it."

"Of course," said the other Mildew with a smile. "You are such a—"

Mildew had chosen a particularly dusty corner of the trophy room in which to hide, and some of that dust now wandered into his nostrils, and though he tried very hard to stop himself, he had no choice but to sneeze loudly.

"Eeeek!" squeaked Sponge, hopping into the air and knocking into the other Mildew.

Mildew, peeking from behind the cabinet, saw very clearly that as Sponge knocked the other Mildew, the other Mildew knocked the plinth on which the Spoon rested on a crimson velvet cushion and it slid off—and into the other Mildew's pocket.

The two boys hurried from the room. Mildew smiled to himself.

So I was the mysterious sneezer, he thought. *As well as the mysterious Spoon thief!*

Mildew reached into his pocket, expecting to find the Spoon there, then realized that he was not wearing the same clothes as he had been when the Spoon fell into his jacket. Those clothes were lying in shreds back in the Viking village.

Curses, thought Mildew. *The School Spoon is stranded back in the Viking age.*

Mildew resolved then and there that he would go back in time again, find himself at the Viking village, and bring the Spoon back.

Wait a minute! thought Mildew. *Of course. I must do exactly that—for I saw myself doing that very thing when I was tied to the post. So I didn't really desert myself in my hour of need—I already knew my head was safe!*

Mildew waited for the other Mildew and Sponge to move away before setting off back to the time machine. He whizzed back to the Viking village, went to where he was tied to a post, rummaged around in his own pocket for the School Spoon, and returned triumphant to Maudlin Towers, adjusting the dial to arrive back in the present, and headed straight for the trophy room to replace the Spoon. This miracle achieved, Mildew set off to the library with a satisfied swagger to meet his friend Sponge.

"What are you up to?" said Kenningworth as he walked past.

"Up to? Me?" said Mildew. "Nothing. What are you up to, is more like it."

"What am I up to?" said Kenningworth shiftily. "I'm not up to anything."

"Well, then," said Mildew.

"Exactly," said Kenningworth.

The two boys went their separate ways, with one last wary glance over their respective shoulders.

"Sponge!" whispered Mildew as he found his friend in the gloomiest corner of the library, deeply engrossed in a large and ancient-looking book. "I have had such an adventure!" So Mildew told Sponge all about how he had inadvertently been sent back to the Viking age and had been about to be sacrificed when he had passed out and awoken to find himself smelling of damp dog with his clothes ripped to shreds, and how he had then escaped to become the supposedly ghostly Viking they had seen in the ha-ha three days ago, and how he had seen himself accidentally steal the School Spoon and then had gone back in time to retrieve the Spoon from himself and return to the present to put it back.

"I say, Mildew," said Sponge. "You are frightfully clever. And now that the School Spoon is back in its rightful place, all will be well again."

"Indeed."

"You're a hero, Mildew."

"I suppose I am, Sponge. Although only you will ever know."

"Yes—of course. We can't tell, can we?"

"No one would believe us if we did, Sponge."

The two boys chuckled and mused on this and other aspects of Mildew's escapade as they walked through the school.

"I think we should go and make a special visit to the School Spoon," said Sponge. "By way of a private celebration."

"Excellent idea, Sponge," said Mildew.

And so they made their way to the trophy room.

"But I don't understand, Mildew," said Sponge when they walked into the room and were faced with a total absence of Spoon. "I thought you said that—"

"It's not possible," said Mildew. "I put it back! I put it back! But it's gone! Gone. How is that possible, Sponge?"

"There, there, boys," said the Headmaster, suddenly appearing behind them. "I know it's hard to take, but we must be strong. How is your piece about the life of the school going, Mildew?"

"My what?" said Mildew. "Oh—very well, sir. We're still gathering research."

"Very good, very good," said the Headmaster. "I'm amazed that you have the time to do this and rehearse for the you-know-what."

The Headmaster winked at Mildew, and it took Mildew a moment to remember about the play he'd invented when he was still dressed as a Viking.

"It has been tiring, sir," said Mildew.

"Rehearsing?" said Sponge. "Ow!"

"Shh," said Mildew. "We don't want to spoil the surprise, do we?"

The Headmaster winked at Mildew again and walked away, chuckling to himself.

"You kicked me, Mildew," said Sponge. "And it hurt."

"I'm sorry, old friend," said Mildew. "It had to be done."

"And what was all that about rehearsing?"

"I'll explain later," said Mildew, pulling at his own hair in exasperation. "Right now we have to work out what madness has occurred. How on earth has the School Spoon disappeared again? I did not risk having my head lopped off for nothing. Come on, Sponge."

16

Two Distinct Noises, Neither of Them Good

Mildew and Sponge had never thought about anything quite so hard as they thought about the whereabouts of the School Spoon.

They thought and thought, had a little rest while their brains caught their breaths, and then thought some more.

But no inspiration came, and the two boys sighed and slumped onto a bench, exhausted.

"You never did tell me what you did to your arm," said Sponge.

"I have tried, to be fair," said Mildew. "If you weren't so sensitive about blood—I mean soup—I'd have told you long before now."

"Well, tell me now. I shall try to be brave," said Sponge.

"Very well. It is quite an interesting story. It all started when my beloved parents decided that it would be easier for them if they dropped me off at school on their way to see the McMildews of Scotland. So instead of getting a week off for the fall holidays, I only got a long weekend before they dumped me back here on the Wednesday afternoon."

"How awful," said Sponge. "What did you do?"

"Well, what could I do?" said Mildew. "I simply had to make the best of it."

"Was there anyone about?"

"Hardly anyone," said Mildew. "Flintlock. The Headmaster. A couple of the teachers. No boys at all."

"It must have been awfully dull."

"It was," admitted Mildew. "At first—a bit creepy too. But then there was the most extraordinary occurrence. I was shivering myself to sleep one night, alone in the dorm, when I heard a noise outside."

"A noise?" said Sponge tremulously. "What kind of a noise?"

"There were two distinct noises, neither of them good," said Mildew.

Sponge shuddered.

"The first was the scream of a young girl," said Mildew.

"But there aren't any young girls at Maudlin Towers."

"Precisely."

Sponge shuddered again.

"The second was the howling of some kind of beast."

"A beast, you say?" said Sponge, suddenly alert and peering.

"I do say. And stop peering at me."

"What happened then?"

"Nothing happened for a while," continued Mildew, "and then there were two more noises, neither of which were any better than the first two."

"What were these noises like, Mildew?"

"They came from inside the school now. One was a scampering noise, the other was a kind of snuffling."

"Oh...," said Sponge, shuddering a little more.

"What's more, they were getting closer. I could hear them outside the dorm."

"What did you do?" said Sponge.

"I did what anyone would do in such circumstances, Sponge—I put the sheets over my head and whimpered."

Sponge nodded.

"What happened then?"

"Well, eventually I uncovered my head and strained to detect any noises, but could hear nothing at all. I got out of bed and crept to the door of the dorm, opening it with barely a creak to peer out. I could see nothing at first in the gloom.

"But then the clouds parted and moonlight flooded in from the skylight above the stairwell, and something rushed toward me and struck me, scratching my arm and knocking me to the floor. I lay there dazed."

Sponge shuddered.

"Was there a lot of … ?"

"Soup?" said Mildew. "I'm afraid there was. A couple of ladlefuls at least."

"How awful," said Sponge.

"Then I heard a bang and something dropped down beside me."

"Gosh," said Sponge. "What was it?"

"Well, that's just it," said Mildew. "I must have banged my head when I fell because the next thing I knew I was in the sickroom at the mercy of Mrs. Leecham, and try as I might, I haven't been able to see these things clearly since. The thing on the stairs and whatever fell down beside me are thrown into deep shadow whenever I try to bring them to mind."

"Try, Mildew," implored Sponge. "Try harder."

Mildew frowned with concentration, but shook his head.

"It's no good," he said after a moment. "I thought I had it there, but it's gone again."

"How frustrating!" said Sponge. "I wonder if the mysterious intruder you saw has anything to do with the theft of the School Spoon."

"Hmmm. Good point. We hadn't thought about the thief coming from outside the school. That's only going to make it harder to find out who it is."

"It must have been a troubling few days for the Headmaster," said Sponge. "What with you being injured and then old Particle biting the dust."

"But that's it!" cried Mildew. "That's who was lying beside me. I remember now! It was Mr. Particle. What's more, his clothes were all ripped and torn and covered in…soup. Unless I'm mistaken, he was a little past the verge of being dead."

"Dead?" said Sponge.

"Exceptionally."

Sponge tried not to think about the soup. He frowned and stroked his chin. Mildew was still frowning with concentration, trying to remember more of what took place.

"Good grief!" said Mildew. "It's coming back to me now. But it can't be. And yet…"

"What?" said Sponge.

"At first Particle wasn't Particle at all…He was a wolf!"

"A wolf?" said Sponge.

"I'm afraid so," said Mildew. "Fur and teeth and all. It's an odd coincidence, isn't it? That the Vikings should have their wolf obsession and then—"

"Wait a minute!" said Sponge. "His clothes were ripped—and your clothes were all ripped and torn when you awoke in that Viking village?"

"Yes," said Mildew. "But I don't see what that's—"

"And didn't you say you heard scampering and snuffling outside the door?"

"I did, but—"

"And wasn't there a full moon in the Viking village and a full moon just before you were attacked that night—when you saw the intruder on the stairs?"

"Yes, but—"

"But don't you see?" said Sponge.

"Not really, no."

"You're a werewolf boy!"

"A werewolf boy? Have you gone mad, Sponge?"

"I don't think so. Come with me!"

Sponge took Mildew to the same dingy corner of the library Mildew had found him in previously. Sponge took a large, dusty volume from the shelf and flicked through the pages, making them both cough.

"You see! Look!"

Sponge pointed to a series of ancient wood-engraved illustrations showing a boy being attacked by a wolf standing on its hind legs.

"A werewolf!" whispered Sponge solemnly.

"It never ceases to surprise me that someone of your nervous disposition reads such things, Sponge."

"I can't stop myself."

Another image showed the werewolf being shot dead. Yet another showed a transformation scene in which the boy who'd been attacked was now himself turning into a wolf.

"Do you see the full moon?" said Sponge. "That's the trigger for the change."

"I see what you're saying," said Mildew. "But do you really mean to say that I was attacked by a werewolf?"

"I can see no other explanation," said Sponge. "Particle must have been a werewolf and the curse has been passed on to you through those scratches on your arm. That's what happens, you see. It's like a disease. You must have changed to a werewolf that night in the Viking village and loosened the bonds with your wolfish superstrength."

Mildew flicked a few pages ahead in the book.

"Where is the part where it mentions a cure?" he said.

Sponge turned back and pointed to the were-wolf being shot.

"I'm afraid that appears to be the only cure," said Sponge. "A silver bullet."

Mildew's legs felt weaker than usual.

"But how on earth did old Particle become a werewolf?" said Mildew.

"Don't you recall how, at the end of last term, Particle returned from a trip to Bohemia with those nasty gashes in his face?"

"I do, Sponge," said Mildew. "He told us he'd cut himself shaving. Thinking back now, that did seem unlikely. Unless he'd been shaving with a rake."

"I think Particle had been attacked by a were-wolf on his trip to Bohemia and had returned to become a werewolf himself every full moon. He must have changed on one of his trips to the Viking village and caused havoc while he was there. That's who they were trying to appease with your sacrifice."

"I was being sacrificed to Mr. Particle?" said Mildew.

"In a way," said Sponge.

"But how did he keep it a secret?" said Mildew.

"He must have recovered and gotten back to Maudlin Towers somehow. I suppose he took himself off to the hills when he felt an attack coming on. Don't you remember the local sheep farmers complaining there was a mad dog on the loose last term?"

"Yes," said Mildew. "That's right. As a matter of fact, when I arrived here during the fall holidays, a group of farmers turned up saying the dog had been seen returning to the school grounds. It was old Particle himself who told them that it was impossible—that there was no dog, mad or otherwise, in Maudlin Towers."

"No dog—but there was a wolf!" said Sponge.

"And then the old sheep-worrier went and attacked me!" said Mildew. "I've a good mind to inform the school board and have him dismissed."

"And one could hardly blame you, Mildew," said Sponge. "But sadly the old fellow is dead."

"Shame," said Mildew. "And not from a sudden illness, as the Headmaster told us, but from a sudden bullet to the ticker."

"A silver bullet," said Sponge.

"Indeed. Which means that the Headmaster was in on it. Maybe he even shot him."

Sponge shook his head.

"I think that was Flintlock. If you remember, he's been patrolling the grounds with a gun for weeks."

The thought of Flintlock and a silver-bullet-loaded rifle made Mildew's knees wobble.

"How long before I'm gnawing mutton on the moors, Sponge? How long before he's after me with that gun?"

"Yes," said Sponge. "I wonder why they let you go when you had been injured? They must know that's how a werewolf passes on the werewolfness. What did they do when they found you?"

"They took me to the sickroom and Leecham bandaged me up. I had a frightful pain in my head too. And a big lump."

"Curious," said Sponge.

Mildew's southernmost lip began to quiver.

"But I don't want to die," said Mildew. "I'm too young. There are so many things I have yet to achieve."

"Quite," said Sponge. "But all is not hopeless. I have an idea."

The Scream of a Young Girl

Mildew listened to his friend's plan, then opened his mouth to speak, but his brain had mislaid the words he had hoped to use and he closed it again. After a moment he opened it again and this came out…

"So you are suggesting that we use the time machine to go back in time and save me from Particle before he attacks me?"

"Precisely," said Sponge.

"But if he doesn't attack me then I won't become a werewolf boy, will I, which means I'll still be tied to the post in the Viking village ahead of getting my head chopped off. And the worst of it is, Sponge, I could have saved myself when I came to get the Spoon. Instead of which I deserted myself in my hour of need."

Mildew's upper lip began to lose some of its structural integrity.

"Don't worry," said Sponge. "I've thought of that too."

"You have?" said Mildew.

"Yes," said Sponge. "Leave that to me."

"To you?" said Mildew doubtfully.

Sponge tried to ignore this doubting of his abilities.

"I think it's better that I go back in time this time, Mildew."

"How so?"

"Because I think you have been very confused by your multiple selves, and also I'd quite like to have a go on the time machine."

"Very well," said Mildew. "That seems only fair."

The two boys headed off to the bothy.

"First I will go back to the night of the attack by Mr. Particle. We should only need to move the dial a slight amount…Do you see in the notebook? Mr. Luckless makes a note of where the dial was when he gained possession of the time machine. That must have been very shortly after Particle kicked the bucket. So just before then should be perfect."

"Must we go back to that?" said Mildew. "I'm not sure I could bear to do it again."

"You won't be doing it again, Mildew," said Sponge. "I'm the one going back, remember? And it will be a first for me as I wasn't there the first time."

"You always were better at science than I, Sponge."

"It will all be well," said Sponge.

With Mildew looking on, Sponge took his position in the chair. Mildew showed him how to work the dial and Sponge grabbed hold of the lever.

"Bon voy—" said Mildew.

A flash and whine later and Sponge was alone in the bothy. Or so he assumed, because it was pitch dark and he could not see a thing. Standing up, he set off immediately toward the school.

"Eeeeeeeek!!!" screamed Sponge as he fell headlong into the ha-ha.

Sponge gathered his scattered wits about him and hurried along the ditch, turning the corner and running toward the school.

The mass of clouds overhead ripped open like moth-eaten trousers to reveal a huge pale moon, full and round. A loud howl rang out in the night.

"Particle!" gasped Sponge to himself. "He'll be changing. There's not a moment to lose!"

Sponge then realized that he himself must have been the girl Mildew had heard screaming outside and blushed.

As he trotted past the shrubbery he noticed a rake leaning against the wall and decided that this might come in handy as a device for keeping werewolves at bay.

Sponge climbed the stairs tentatively, watching every shadow for signs of Mr. Particle, and arrived at the hallway unscathed.

The rake was proving to be heavier and more cumbersome than he'd ever imagined, and he was unable to carry it any longer and was forced to drag it behind him down the hallway. He heard a distinct whimper from inside the dorm.

"Mildew!" whispered Sponge to himself.

He then became aware of a strange odor creeping up the stairwell. He sniffed and sniffed, trying to imagine what it might be.

It was some kind of animal, he thought. A dog, perhaps? No—something like a dog…A wolf! It was the changed Mr. Particle coming up the stairs. Sponge could barely stop himself from squealing and hurried off to the end of the hallway to hide, as stealthily as a small boy could whilst holding a rake.

Just as Mildew had told him, his friend appeared at the dormitory door and edged out onto the landing, peering down into the stairwell, when the moon burst through the skylight and the now-changed Particle howled and bounded up the stairs, clearly intent on savaging poor Mildew.

Sponge leaped into action, swinging the rake with all his might but with an inaccuracy for which he was renowned.

He missed the werewolf entirely and accidentally hit Mildew round the side of the head and raked him on the arm on the swing back, knocking him to the floor. The rake slipped from his grasp and was sent clattering down the landing.

To Sponge's horror, the werewolf now turned its attentions to Sponge. It snarled and growled horribly, baring its huge teeth. It was about to leap when there was an enormous bang and the creature fell down next to Mildew, transforming back into Mr. Particle as the life left its body.

Mildew seemed to come to his senses briefly, turning to look at Mr. Particle before letting out a groan and passing out.

Sponge did not wait for Flintlock and the Headmaster to climb the stairs, but made himself scarce, hiding behind a cupboard at the foot of the attic staircase.

"Should I shoot the boy as well?" Sponge heard Flintlock say. "Just to be on the safe side?"

"Certainly not," said the Headmaster.

"But look—he's been wounded! Infected!" said Flintlock. "Do you want another of these monsters in the school?"

"But he has merely been wounded by this rake," said the Headmaster. "Look."

Flintlock peered at the rake and then at Mildew and reluctantly lowered his gun.

"What on earth a rake is doing here, heaven only knows," said the Headmaster. "You take Mr. Particle and I'll take Mildew to the sickroom. We shall say Mr. Particle died of a sudden illness."

"What if the boy saw something?" said Flintlock.

"He didn't see anything, Mr. Flintlock," said the Headmaster. "He is quite unconscious. But quickly—off with Mr. Particle before Mildew wakes up."

Mr. Flintlock put his gun on his back, lifted Mr. Particle as though he were nothing more than a sack of cats and threw him over his shoulder, while the Headmaster staggered after him down the stairs, carrying Mildew in his arms.

So Mildew never was scratched by the werewolf, thought Sponge. *But then what happened at the Viking village?*

There was only one way to find out.

With that thought, Sponge slipped quietly down the back stairs and out of the school, to return to the bothy and the time machine.

Spudge

S ponge set the dial of the time machine to the place marked by Mr. Particle in the book to denote what they now knew was the Viking village, and was about to pull the lever when he had a sudden thought.

With great effort he moved the time machine a chair's breadth to the right and then, sitting down again, he pulled the lever. A flash and a whine later and Sponge blinked out on a very different scene.

He was sitting in the corner of a very pleasant courtyard with potted plants, a small statue on a plinth, and a well in the center. He recognized the scene immediately from Mr. Luckless's detailed description of it, and it now dawned on him that he had not arrived in a Viking village, but had gone back to Roman times instead.

He was about to move the dial to the other marked place when it occurred to him that this was too good an opportunity to miss. He had always been interested in the Roman age, and Mr. Luckless's vivid evocation of it had only increased that interest. Surely he could just have a little look around before popping back—forward—to see Mildew?

Sponge had moved the time machine sideways because he was worried that the two machines might superimpose themselves or blow up or some such if they occupied the same space. This precaution had been made because he knew Mildew had a time machine in the Viking period.

But now Sponge could see that there was another time machine standing next to his, and this could mean only one thing: that old Luckless was here as well.

There was a partition wall pierced here and there with holes in a decorative pattern and this allowed Sponge to both hide and, at one and the same time, peep—the very best kind of hiding there was.

Sure enough, after a moment or three, Mr. Luckless appeared in the midst of a great commotion. Miss Livia was causing a mighty to-do, weeping and wailing and waving her arms about like a malfunctioning windmill.

Mr. Luckless was desperately trying to extricate himself from the squid-like grip of Miss Livia, but the more he tried to get away, the more her tentacles seemed to wrap themselves mercilessly around the poor teacher's person.

"Livia!" said Mr. Luckless. "Please! I must insist! I will return as soon as I can, but I have the boys to think of."

With that Mr. Luckless pulled himself free and Miss Livia hurled a volley of Latin curses before flouncing away. Mr. Luckless's resolve seemed to fail him for a moment and he looked as though he was about to follow her, but then he shook his head and marched off toward the time machine, with Sponge following him behind the pierced wall.

When Mr. Luckless saw the extra time machine he put his hand to his forehead and stared in amazement. He looked around, making Sponge duck down, and muttered to himself. He carried on muttering and holding his head for some time, before finally sitting in the nearest time machine and flashing and whining himself into the future.

Sponge felt sorry for Mr. Luckless—giving up Miss Livia out of a sense of duty to the boys of Maudlin Towers. Sponge wondered if they were quite worthy of such selfless devotion.

Clearly Sponge had arrived on one of Mr. Luckless's earlier visits—a visit previous to the one in which Miss Livia would launch herself lapward to be flashed into the future where she would curdle Enderpenny's blood with her attic wailing and subsequently take up her post as Latin tutor.

Sponge wondered if it might not be the best idea to head off now before he did something to confuse things even more, as seemed to be the norm with this time travel nonsense.

Then Sponge noticed a cloud shadow pass over him and looked up to see that the cloud wasn't a cloud at all but a burly Roman type who grabbed Sponge by the scruff of the neck and frog-marched him toward the villa.

Sponge wished he'd paid more attention in his Latin classes because the Roman servant was saying a great many things, and without understanding them, Sponge had the distinct impression that a great many of these things were threats.

Eventually Sponge was delivered to Miss Livia, who listened to the servant's grumblings as he pushed Sponge forward. Miss Livia looked Sponge up and down and clearly recognized a similarity in his and Mr. Luckless's clothing.

"Few. Churr," she said, carefully and bafflingly.

"I beg your pardon?" said Sponge. "My Latin isn't quite what it might be. I'm sure you'll do a much better job than our last Latin teacher, Mr. Particle. I know it's wrong to speak ill of the departed but he was absolutely—"

"Few. Churr," she repeated, with some effort and not a little pride.

And then Sponge realized what she was saying.

"Ah—future. You're saying 'future.' Yes—I am from the future. Like old Luckless."

"Luck. Lass?"

"Indeed," said Sponge. "Tall chap. Prone to getting a little flummoxed, but a thoroughly decent sort of—"

"Lenn. Nudd."

Sponge did have a dim recollection that Lenn-nudd—or, rather, Leonard—was Mr. Luckless's first name.

"Lenn-nudd, yes," said Sponge. "He is my history teacher. In the few-churr."

"Tea. Churr," she said, nodding. "Tea. Churr."

This was going to be an exhausting conversation, thought Sponge, although he had to admit that Miss Livia's English was considerably better

158

than his Latin. He wondered how many days Mr. Luckless had actually spent in Miss Livia's company for her to have such a grasp of the language. Sponge thought he ought to try and introduce himself. He pointed to his chest.

"Sponge," he said.

Miss Livia smiled and nodded.

"Spudge," she replied.

"Not quite," he said. "Sponge."

"Spudge," she repeated.

"Almost," said Sponge. "Try again. Sponge. Spunnnnnnge."

"Spudge," said Miss Livia again, and this time accompanied it with a little frown.

"Close enough," said Sponge with a sigh.

Miss Livia pointed to herself.

"Livia," she said.

"Livia," agreed Sponge. "Although I'd feel more comfortable if we stuck to Miss Livia."

Miss Livia chuckled and clapped her hands, delighted that Sponge had learned to say her name so quickly. She waved her scowling servant away and ushered Sponge inside.

There on the floor was the mosaic Mr. Luckless had so carefully described, and if anything it was even more impressive than he had led them to believe.

In fact, the whole villa was as cheerful as Maudlin Towers was gloom-laden. The walls were painted in rich colors and there were decorative pots and statues and plants everywhere.

"You. Like. Here?" Miss Livia managed to get out after much frowning and a few false starts.

"Oh yes," said Sponge. "It's lovely. Beautiful. *Bella*."

Miss Livia beamed.

"You. Stay!" she announced.

"Well, I'm not really sure about that," said Sponge. "I think I do have to get back. I'm not really supposed to be here at all as a matter of fact. I'm supposed to be saving my chum from becoming a werewolf…"

Miss Livia frowned with a very compelling kind of fierceness, and Sponge suddenly felt compelled to be quiet and stay.

Spudge to the Rescue

Sponge was invited to sit on a couch and eat grapes, which the servant, Spatula, reluctantly brought to him on a silver platter.

Miss Livia sat down on another couch and smiled at him, clearly trying to formulate some kind of a conversation opener in her mind.

"You. Like. Here?" she said with some effort eventually.

Sponge looked around and, trying to ignore the scowling Spatula, he said, "Yes—it's very nice."

"Nice," said Miss Livia with a smile. "Yes. Nice."

"I like the under-floor heating," said Sponge. "I wish we had it at Maudlin Towers."

Miss Livia's eyebrows fluttered up and down and her mouth underwent a series of confused openings and closings. This outburst of Sponge's appeared to be too much for her. A silence ensued during which Sponge twiddled his thumbs nervously.

This awkwardness went on for some time until it was suddenly relieved by the arrival of a messenger, who entered, bowed, and handed Miss Livia a piece of bark or some such, on which something was written. Whatever it was that the note contained, it was clearly troubling news and Miss Livia got up and followed the messenger into the courtyard, where there ensued a long conversation.

Sponge got up and wandered about, looking at the various figures described in the mosaic and almost knocking over and smashing a rather expensive-looking glass vase.

I think it might be safer if I wander about outside, he thought.

Sponge could see that Miss Livia and the messenger were still earnestly conversing by the well.

It was chilly in the courtyard. A cold wind was blowing and storm clouds were building up over Pug's Peak. As Sponge watched them billowing like black smoke, he saw a flash of lightning hit the summit, followed by a distant rumble of thunder. There was an almost imperceptible shudder in the crag face and then a tiny fragment of rock, no bigger than a raisin, broke away from the summit and began to slide and then bounce its way down.

Sponge watched the progress of the tiny piece of rock with a kind of relaxed indifference, until somewhere in the back of his mind he began, for some reason, to recall a recent art lesson with Mr. Riddell.

What was that called? When something was small only because it was far away? Perplexing? No—perspective, that was it!

He thought to himself that had he been on the top of Pug's Peak, he would have appeared even tinier than the tiny rock that was even now looking a trifle larger as it bounced down the hillside.

In fact, Sponge surmised he would have been much, much smaller and therefore, if his understanding of the concept of perspective was correct (and he thought it was) then the rock must be much, much larger than he was—and it appeared to be heading their way rather quickly.

Sponge walked toward Miss Livia, who was sending the messenger away, wondering what the words for "Look out!" were in Latin. Was it *prospeculor*? *Prospeculari*? Perhaps he should just say "danger." Now what was that in Latin?

He wished he had paid more attention in his lessons, but there was nothing he could do about that. Sponge coughed to catch Miss Livia's attention.

"Excuse me," he said, grabbing hold of her arm. "If you could just move this way for a moment."

Miss Livia raised a confused eyebrow.

"Danger," said Sponge by way of explanation.

He pushed Miss Livia sideways just as the rock, now the size of a curled-up elephant, slammed into the floor of the courtyard after having bounced over the wall.

"You see?" said Sponge. "Danger. *Periculum.* Is that right?"

Miss Livia stared wide-eyed and Spatula rushed forward, making Sponge back off fearfully. But the grinning servant embraced him as though Sponge were his long-lost son.

"*Gratia!*" he cried.

"Oh—that means thanks, doesn't it?" said Sponge. "Well, you're very welcome, I'm sure."

No sooner had Spatula released him than Miss Livia took over, hugging Sponge to the point of suffocation. Sponge was greeted by the whole household as a hero.

Before Sponge knew what was happening, Miss Livia called out some orders and a sleepy-looking man in an apron and carrying a hammer and chisel appeared. Livia pointed to Sponge and, after a short conversation, the man nodded and indicated for Sponge to follow.

In another courtyard were sculptures in varying states of completion, and it became clear that Sponge was being asked to pose for a bust that the sculptor had already roughly hewn from a block of marble.

I'm a hero, thought Sponge. *I am to be immortalized.*

The sculptor peered at Sponge, and Sponge, suddenly remembering the marble bust Flintlock had found in the school grounds, tried to emulate the heroic set of its jaw.

The sculptor started work, constantly peering round and over the marble block to look at Sponge, his arms a blur of activity, the sound of his chisel chattering frantically and a spray of chips and dust flying everywhere.

The whole process was rather alarming for Sponge and made it hard for him to keep the heroic expression. In a surprisingly short amount of time, the sculptor turned the sculpture round with a flourish and a smile, and there it was—the very bust that Flintlock had dug up centuries later!

"I'm honored!" said Sponge, and he was.

Sponge was very honored indeed to be preserved for posterity in this way and shook the sculptor's hand warmly in appreciation.

But the heroic set of the marble Sponge's jaw reminded him that he had a job to do.

What am I doing? he thought. *I have allowed myself to be distracted. I must get back—or is it forward?—to Mildew!*

Keeping his firm jaw in place, Sponge asserted himself and told Miss Livia that he simply must go.

"You. Go. Few. Churr?" she said a little sadly.

"Yes," said Sponge. "I'm afraid so. Not that I haven't enjoyed myself tremendously."

He took his seat in the time machine, adjusted the dial, and, remembering his manners, added, "Thanks for having me," before pulling the lever.

20

Sponge to the Rescue

When Sponge arrived in the Viking village, he was pleased to see that his moving-the-chair-slightly-sideways precaution had worked again and that Mildew had clearly had the same idea, for the three time machines—Sponge's, Mildew's, and the Other Mildew's—now sat alongside each other, meaning that once he had left to return to the future, there would still be one for Mildew to use.

Where it had been the middle of the night back at Maudlin Towers and daytime in Roman times, it was evening in Viking times, but it was getting darker by the minute. Sponge set off in search of Mildew, to save him from the sacrificial ax.

As he sneaked toward the center of the village, he could see the glow of a bonfire and hear the singing of Viking songs, no doubt celebrating the impending doom of his friend. Passing one of the feast tables, Sponge grabbed a large knife and took cover behind one of the huts nearby.

He peered out and saw poor Mildew tied to the post. He was about to go over and untie his friend when he spotted another figure heading in the same direction.

"Mildew!" whispered Sponge to himself.

For it was indeed he. Or the other he. The other Mildew, coming back from the future to take the School Spoon from his own pocket. Despite the tied-up Mildew's protestations, the other Mildew left without a backward glance.

"Wait!" cried the bound Mildew before breaking into sobbing and plaintive mutterings.

Sponge saw his chance and scurried forward with the knife. Mildew evidently could not see it was Sponge coming to his assistance and cried out in panic, falling immediately into a faint.

Sponge was about to cut through Mildew's ropes when he heard a noise from behind and turned: a boy about his own age was staggering toward him, moaning and clutching his head.

"Uh-oh!" said Sponge and panicked, dropping the knife.

The boy looked up with red-rimmed eyes and

saw Sponge, glanced between him and the bound Mildew, clearly very surprised to see another strangely dressed boy in the village.

Then he grinned, and there was something so unpleasant about the grin that Sponge looked down at the knife on the ground between them, rather wishing it were in his hand. The boy was quicker, and in a flash, Sponge saw the knife being thrust toward him.

But Sponge could see that the boy, who looked decidedly ill, was merely threatening him, for he made it clear from his movements and expression that he wanted Sponge's jacket.

This must have been the boy Mildew described as being so very interested in Mildew's clothes.

Sponge needed no further persuasion and took his jacket off and handed it to the boy, who shed his own ragged tunic and replaced it with Sponge's school blazer. As he did so, Sponge noticed a vicious-looking wound on his arm.

The boy stood in Sponge's blazer, staring admiringly down at himself.

He then looked at Sponge's trousers.

"Now see here," said Sponge. "A fellow can't just go about taking another fellow's trousers."

The boy took a step forward, but as he did so, the moon suddenly burst through the clouds and he was shaken by violent spasms and sank to his knees, dropping the knife and moaning and growling.

Sponge saw his opportunity and retreated to the cover of a small but very pungent dung heap and peeked out.

The boy shook and twitched and convulsed and Sponge looked on in confusion and dread as Mildew lolled limply against the post, still in a faint.

Sponge looked on aghast as, by the ghostly light of the moon, he saw the boy raise himself up, staring at his own hands as they contorted and changed, as his arms grew and bulged, splitting open the sleeves of Sponge's jacket and leaving them frayed and tattered.

It was a mark of the enormity of the horror that Sponge gave not a second's thought to what his mother would have to say about that ripped blazer.

So you're the werewolf boy! he thought.

He stood, spellbound, watching from behind the dung heap as the boy's head and face underwent a series of bizarre changes, the nose and jaw extruding into a long snout and pointed ears forming on his head, the whole now covered in gray fur.

Sponge gasped.

The werewolf boy, his hearing as sharp as his teeth, turned instantly at the sound, sniffing at the air for any hint of where it had come from. But though he peered into the gloom with his keen wolf eyes, the stink of the dung heap was enough to conceal Sponge's scent. Sponge almost fainted with relief.

But he had no time to faint. The werewolf boy was turning his attention to Mildew, edging toward him, sniffing hungrily. The creature raised its head to the heavens and howled long and loud and then flew at Mildew with its clawed hands, shredding through the ropes and his clothes.

"No!" shouted Sponge.

The werewolf boy turned angrily to face him. Sponge picked up a rock at his feet and hurled it with all his poorly aimed might, hitting Mildew square on the fore- head just as he was coming round.

The creature snarled and bounded off toward the center of the village, the villagers all having secured themselves safely inside their huts.

No one attempted to stop the werewolf boy.

They must think of him as sacred, thought Sponge. Mildew was a sacrifice to appease the wolf god and the Viking villagers were simply going to keep themselves safe until the werewolf boy had gone.

While the werewolf boy went on the rampage, howling and leaping up onto the tables to eat the food prepared for the feast, Sponge went over to check on his friend, who was still unconscious, a large bump forming on his forehead. But he was otherwise unharmed, the claws of the werewolf boy mercifully not having reached his skin.

"Thank goodness!" said Sponge. "Mildew is unharmed. Apart from that bump on his head. But never mind…"

Sponge then heard the werewolf boy returning and ran back to his dung heap, ensuring this time that he stood in the midst of it for maximum effect.

The werewolf boy sniffed at Mildew once or twice but had presumably eaten his fill at the feast and, with one more tired-sounding howl, he bounded off up what Sponge now realized was Pug's Peak.

The Viking chief and the villagers advanced on Mildew, who was blearily coming round. But when they saw his tattered jacket and cut bonds, they all stepped back, aghast, presumably assuming Mildew to be a werewolf boy, and mistaking Mildew's shredded blazer for Sponge's tattered blazer as worn by the real werewolf boy. The boy they had intended to sacrifice to the werewolf boy was himself a werewolf. They were clearly eager to appease the mighty wolf god and a little perplexed as to what to do next. The chief whispered instructions to those around him.

Before Sponge could understand what was going on, the villagers all howled in mimicry of the werewolf, handed Mildew new clothes, the helmet and ax, and began to carry him through the village in triumphant procession.

Sponge saw that there was really no more for him to do now—everything was taking place just as Mildew had related and Mildew would return safe and sound and helmeted—and so Sponge headed off back to the time machine.

The other Mildew's machine was now gone—as that Mildew had made his way back to school with the Spoon—and Sponge sat down in his, set the dial for Maudlin Towers, and pulled the lever.

Sponge Returns from the Dung Heap

A flash and a whine brought Sponge back to Maudlin Towers and the present, and there standing in front of him in the dimly lit bothy was Mildew.

"Great news," said Sponge as he stood up from the time machine. "You were never a werewolf boy, Mildew. You were scratched by a rake."

"But how? And where's your jacket, Sponge? And what's that awful smell?"

"My jacket was stolen by the real werewolf boy and I've been standing in a dung heap."

"What on earth…"

"That's not the half of it…"

Sponge set about telling Mildew (almost) all about his trip back to the night when Mildew was attacked by the Particle werewolf, his journey to the Roman villa and his further adventures in the Viking village, and the tattered-blazer-related case of mistaken identity.

"So when I thought I'd seen you, I had?" said Mildew. "My old friend. You didn't mention how I came to suffer that blow to the head."

"That remains a mystery," said Sponge.

Mildew nodded.

"And you say I received my wound from a rake. How on earth did that happen?"

"That, too, remains a puzzle."

Mildew peered suspiciously at Sponge, who stared intently at the backs of his own hands. He frowned.

"So do you think old Particle caught his werewolfery on a trip back to Viking times and not on his trip to Bohemia?" said Mildew.

"That's possible," said Sponge. "But I rather think it might be the other way round."

"How so?"

"I wonder if, on a trip back to Viking times, old Particle was, in fact, the one who infected that unfortunate Viking boy."

"You could be right."

"He may have started a whole chain of werewolf infections," said Sponge, "that went on and on through time. Perhaps leading to the very werewolf attack he suffered himself."

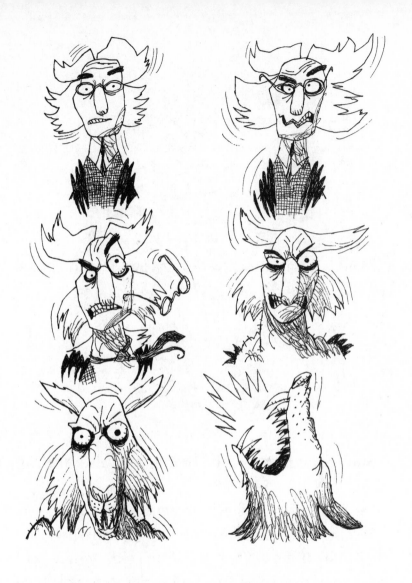

"So in a way he might be responsible for his own terrible end?"

"Yes," said Sponge. "It makes one think, doesn't it?"

"It makes one's brain wince, that's for sure."

Sponge nodded. His brain was also feeling tender.

"So remind me, where are we now, Sponge?"

"Well, the School Spoon is still missing, the Christmas holidays are still canceled, we are still enrolled in the Hill-Running Tournament, you have invented a fictitious play which the Headmaster is expecting us to perform, as well as a piece you are writing for the school newspaper, and Miss Livia is still wandering about in the present."

"So what have we actually achieved?"

"We know that the ghost in the ha-ha was, in fact, you, and that the ghost in the attic was Miss Livia, but aside from that I'm not sure. We do seem to have added calamities to those we already faced."

Mildew groaned and put his head in his hands.

"What are we to do, Sponge?"

"I wish I knew."

"I blame an awful lot of this on that infernal time machine," said Mildew.

Sponge nodded.

"It does seem to be the source of a great many of our present problems. But on the other hand it may also be the source of their solutions."

"No!" said Mildew. "Every time we go anywhere in that thing we seem to make things worse. We need to persuade Mr. Luckless to take his Roman lady back to Roman times, and then it must be destroyed."

"Destroyed?"

"Yes—destroyed. We aren't meant to see the past, Sponge. That's why historians are always insane."

Sponge peered at Mildew.

"Yes—but what about the future?"

"What about it?" said Mildew.

"Have you never wondered about the future?"

"Of course," said Mildew. "Who hasn't? Will we have steam-driven horses, that kind of thing."

"Well, then?" said Sponge, waggling his eyebrows up and down and grinning.

"Well, what?"

"Why don't we take one last spin in the time machine and have a look?" said Sponge.

"Do you think that's wise?" said Mildew. "And how will it help us solve our present predicaments regarding the Spoon and the Yuletide holidays and such?"

"Oh, it won't," said Sponge. "This would be purely recreational—I mean educational."

"We would be explorers," said Mildew.

"In a way," agreed Sponge. "Bold adventurers."

"Let's do it!" cried Mildew. "To the future!"

Two in a Time Machine

The boys stood looking at the time machine, wondering how to phrase the question on both their minds.

"How exactly are we both to fit?" asked Sponge.

"Yes—I was also wondering that," said Mildew.

"Miss Livia—" began Sponge.

"There will be no lap-sitting, Sponge," said Mildew. "Put that out of your mind once and for all. It's simply not dignified or proper."

"Of course," said Sponge. "You're right, of course."

"I wonder if such drastic steps are necessary in any case," said Mildew. "I think we might both fit onto that seat if we were to sit at precisely the same time."

"Hmmm," said Sponge. "I think you may be right."

They got into position, backs to the chair, bottoms to the seat.

"On the count of three," said Mildew.

"On the three or after the three?" said Sponge.

"On," said Mildew. "One. Two. Three!"

Both boys sat down and squished into the grip of the chair's leather arms. Sponge groaned slightly.

"It's not very comfortable, is it?"

"Explorers don't bother about a bit of discomfort," said Mildew.

"Perhaps they have slimmer friends," said Sponge.

Mildew scowled but chose not to respond to this slur.

"Time travel seems to have had a curious effect on you, Sponge," said Mildew. "I hope things will return to normal when we have seen the last of this machine."

"How far into the future shall we go?" said Sponge, ignoring Mildew's scowl.

"Oh, I don't know," said Mildew. "Far enough for it to be very, very different from this layer of tedium in which we find ourselves."

"Shall we say a hundred years?" said Sponge.

"Make it a hundred and fifty," said Mildew. "By then we should all be living like kings and riding around in carriages pulled by mechanical horses!"

The boys adjusted the dials and grinned expectantly as they pulled the lever. After the usual flash and flatulent whine, they blinked into the unsuspecting face of the future, where they were surprised to find themselves still inside the bothy.

They squeezed themselves, not without considerable effort, from the chair, opened the door, and stood looking around in amazement at the all too familiar view of Maudlin Towers.

"It's exactly the same," said Sponge disappointedly.

"Well, I suppose it might look the same in a hundred and fifty years," said Mildew. "It was possibly too much to hope for that they'd knock it down. Shall we move the dial a little farther?"

"Well, now that we're here we may as well have a look about," said Sponge. "Let's go inside and see what our forefathers are up to."

"Descendants, Sponge," said Mildew. "Forefathers come before. That's why they're called forefathers."

"Why aren't they called beforefathers? To avoid confusion."

"Some people will always be confused," said Mildew.

"Yes," agreed Sponge. "That's true."

The boys mused on this as they traversed the sports field and entered the school, making for Mr. Luckless's classroom. Or the room that had been Mr. Luckless's one hundred and fifty years previously.

"I don't understand," said Mildew. "How is it possible?"

The classroom was identical to the one they knew. Even the dust looked the same. They heard voices but before they could decide where to hide, in came a group of people.

"Look, Mom," said one of the oddly dressed children at the front—a girl clothed from head to foot in black with a silver ring through one nostril. "They've got people dressed up and everything."

Mildew and Sponge looked around and then realized the child was talking about them.

Hipflask
was here

A woman walked forward and whispered to Sponge, "Lovely to have you here, but why didn't anyone tell me?"

Sponge looked at Mildew and shrugged. The woman clapped her hands and asked the group to come in and gather round.

"As you can see," she said, "we have fashioned this room in exactly the way it looked over a hundred years ago, during the time Maudlin Towers was a school—one of the finest schools in the north of England."

Mildew and Sponge chuckled. The woman cast them a barbed frown.

"Everything is precisely as it was. We have taken a great deal of trouble to ensure that everything is correct right down to the last detail. We even have two of Maudlin Towers' schoolboys with us today."

The group looked at Mildew and Sponge, and the boys performed a small bow.

"Can we, like, talk to them?" said the gloomy girl at the front with the nose ring and black-painted fingernails.

"Of course," said the guide.

"What's your name?" she asked.

"I am Mildew," said Mildew, "of the Berkshire Mildews. And this is my friend Sponge."

"What's your favorite color?"

188

"Blue," said Sponge.

"Ultramarine," said Mildew.

"That is blue," said Sponge.

"A very particular shade of blue, yes."

"But still blue," said Sponge.

"Yes, but some of us—"

"Well," said the guide, raising an eyebrow at the two friends. "Perhaps if we might move on. There's still a lot to see."

The group moved away. A short girl stuck out her tongue at Sponge. The black-clad older girl winked at Mildew. Both boys frowned. Girls were curious creatures.

"What's going on, Sponge?" said Mildew. "What is this place? That girl winked at me, Sponge. Did you see her fingernails? And her nose! Has Maudlin Towers returned to being an asylum?"

"I don't know, Mildew," said Sponge.

"Let's have a little look round," said Mildew.

"Are you sure?" said Sponge. "It seems frightful. There are girls, Mildew. Girls."

"We can't come all this way and only see the inside of Luckless's classroom. Let's explore."

Very Expensive Cookies

The boys opened the door and peered both ways down the corridor. The group and guide had moved off and away. They edged warily out.

"Come on," whispered Mildew, "let's have a look down here." He pointed in the direction of the entrance.

They came at last to the Headmaster's office and peeped inside. It was utterly transformed and they wandered in, dazed and amazed.

It was now full of a very curious array of items—jigsaw puzzles, marmalade, books. Sponge picked up a packet of cookies and began trying to open it.

"Sponge?" said Mildew. "What are you doing?"

"I'm hungry."

"You have to pay for them. This is a shop."

Mildew pointed to a counter with a bored-looking woman reading a book. On the counter was a sign saying PLEASE PAY HERE.

"I don't have any money on me, Mildew. Could I borrow a penny or two?"

Mildew sighed.

"How much are they?"

Sponge looked at the sign on the shelf he'd taken them from. Then he looked at it again. He tapped Mildew on the arm and pointed to it.

"That's impossible," said Mildew. "What sort of fool would pay that much for cookies?"

"I'm just buying some cookies," said a voice nearby.

A woman was holding something to the side of her face and talking to herself loudly. "I'm in the shop."

"Why is she saying that to herself?" asked Sponge. "And why is she saying it so loudly?"

"How on earth should I know?" said Mildew. "Perhaps she is reminding herself where she is."

"I'm looking at the jam," she continued.

The boys looked and, sure enough, she was indeed looking at the jam.

"Curious," said Mildew.

"Wait a minute," she said. "You're breaking up. I'll go outside."

Mildew shook his head.

"The future appears to be even odder and duller than our own time, Sponge."

"With very expensive cookies," said Sponge.

"Indeed," said Mildew.

They contemplated the terrible implications of this for a while until Mildew noticed that the bored-looking woman was now a suspicious-looking woman, despite being the same woman who had always been there.

"Perhaps we had better move on," suggested Mildew.

Sponge readily agreed, with only a swift backward glance at the cookies he had been forced to abandon. They decided to pop into the kitchen in the hope of finding sustenance.

The change in the kitchen was just as startling as

the one in the Headmaster's office, however. They had never seen it so clean and tidy or experienced such a lack of the heady whiff of cabbage.

The pots and pans were polished and ladles sparkled, untroubled by gravy or custard. There seemed to be no actual food at all.

"Look," said Sponge.

"What?"

"The School Spoon," said Sponge.

Sure enough, lying alongside a random collection of other spoons, forks, and knives in a cutlery drawer was the School Spoon. The woman attendant eyed the boys suspiciously.

"It makes you think, doesn't it?" said Sponge.

"Does it?" said Mildew.

"All that fuss about the School Spoon back in our time, and here it is tossed into a cutlery drawer."

"I dare say we will all, in the course of time, be tossed in the cutlery drawer of history, Sponge."

Sponge nodded solemnly.

"Yes, indeed."

The two boys thought about this for a while.

"Wait!" said Sponge.

"What?"

"Why don't we take *this* School Spoon back with us? Then it won't be missing."

"Steal it, you mean?"

"Well, I don't see how it's stealing, Mildew," said Sponge. "After all, we are returning it to its rightful owner. We had it first. In a way, the future has stolen it."

"To be fair to the future, it had already been stolen in the past."

"But it's our past and our Spoon!"

"All true," said Mildew. "You create a diversion."

"What kind of a diver—" began Sponge as Mildew shoved him sideways, making him fall against a table piled with pots and pans, which tipped over, shedding its load noisily on the tiled floor.

"What on earth do you think you're doing?" cried the attendant, pulling Sponge to his feet.

"I'm most terribly sorry," he said, frowning at Mildew. "I appear to have stumbled."

"Look at this mess!" she said. "These things are very old, you know."

Sponge looked at the pans.

"They don't look all that old to me. We have ones in the school kitchen that look exactly the same."

"Very amusing," said the attendant. "I think you may be getting carried away with your roles."

"But I—"

"Shh, Sponge," said Mildew. "We have to get going."

Mildew grabbed him by the arm and pulled him into the corridor.

"You shoved me into a table, Mildew," said Sponge. "I could have hurt myself."

"Yes," said Mildew. "Sorry about that. But I do have the Spoon!"

Mildew waved the Spoon triumphantly.

"Hurrah!" said Sponge.

The boys returned to the bothy, horrified to find the family they had encountered earlier gathered round the time machine. The father was playing with the levers.

"No!" shouted Mildew.

The family and their guide turned to face them.

"I'm afraid you mustn't touch that," said Sponge.

"What is that, anyway?" said the guide. "It's not on my itinerary."

"It's not on your itinerary because it and we are from the past!" said Mildew.

"Are you really from the past?" said the black-clad girl.

Mildew blushed.

"Of course he isn't," said the guide. "And you still haven't told me what that is."

"It's a time machine," said Sponge.

"No, it isn't," said the girl's younger sister.

"Yes, it is!" said Mildew. "How else do you think we got here?"

"By car, I imagine," said the mother.

"What's a car?" said Sponge to Mildew.

"Who cares?" he said. "Come on, Sponge!"

Mildew and Sponge squeezed into the chair and Sponge adjusted the dial.

"To the past!"

Their last view of the future was the aghast faces of the family as, with a flash and a whine, they arrived back in their own time. Or so they hoped.

Lord Maudlin

The two boys blinked their eyes free of the glare from the flash of time travel, got up, and stepped out of the bothy.

There was Maudlin Towers just as they'd left it. Not a welcome sight exactly, but in some ways comfortably familiar. Like a cousin. Or prunes.

They made straight for Mr. Luckless's classroom, eager to shake off the madness they had seen in the future, but instead they found more confusion. For—although they were still in the structure of Mr. Luckless's classroom,—it looked very, very different.

"Well, this is a bit odd," said Sponge.

"It is indeed," said Mildew.

For instead of being filled with the bits and pieces of Mr. Luckless's history classroom—globes and maps and so forth—the room was now filled to indigestion with cabinets and cases filled with stuffed birds. And those birds that couldn't fit in the cabinets perched on top of them on twigs covered in glass domes.

The boys had both seen stuffed animals before, of course—Mildew's own uncle Egbert owned several stuffed sheep—but this flock of deceased warblers was made particularly striking by the fact that each and every one of them wore a little hat—the male of the species wearing a tiny top hat, bowler, or boater, the female, a bite-size bonnet.

Mildew and Sponge were peering into one of the cabinets when they became aware of a strange clanking noise getting louder and louder, as though an armed knight in a full suit of armor was about to walk into the room.

And then an armed knight in a full suit of armor walked into the room. The two boys both remembered Mr. Luckless's comical suggestion of a ghostly knight when the boys had described their upcoming ghost hunt. It didn't seem so comical now.

"Mildew!" cried Sponge, hiding behind his friend, who wished he had been a bit quicker off the mark and hidden behind *his* friend.

They watched in horror as the armored knight lifted his armored arm (accompanied by some painfully high metallic squeaks) and pulled off his helmet with a pop like a champagne cork.

"Aaaargh!" cried Mildew, terrified at what might be revealed.

"Lord Maudlin!" cried Sponge, who had a surprisingly good memory for faces and recognized the uncovered visage as belonging to the benefactor of Maudlin Towers, whose portrait was on the wall in the entrance hall of the school.

"Do I know you?" inquired Lord Maudlin.

"Algernon Spongely-Partwork, sir," said Sponge. "But everyone calls me Sponge. And this is my good friend Arthur Mildew."

"Of the Berkshire Mildews," said Mildew.

Lord Maudlin took off his gauntlet and shook both boys by the hand. Then he peered at them with a grin growing on his face.

"Who are you really?" he asked.

Mildew and Sponge looked at each other.

"It's quite hard to explain, sir," said Sponge.

Lord Maudlin tapped the side of his nose and winked.

"Say no more," he said. "I'll work it out. You've come for tea, I take it?"

"Well—" began Sponge.

"Yes," said Mildew, never one to turn down a chance of cake. "We would be delighted."

"Marvellous. Forecourt! Forecourt!"

A manservant wearing an extraordinary suit of stripes and spots and a look of grim resignation appeared and bowed to them.

"Forecourt," said Lord Maudlin. "My friends and I will be taking tea on the terrace."

"Of course, sir," said Forecourt.

"I see you are admiring Forecourt's costume," said Lord Maudlin. "I designed that myself, didn't I, Forecourt?"

"Yes," said Forecourt. "You certainly did, sir."

There was a weariness in the demeanor of the servant that both boys recognized all too well—the soul-destroying exhaustion of having to pander to the needs of an eccentric grown-up.

Mildew and Sponge followed Lord Maudlin down the corridor toward the main entrance. Sponge couldn't help noticing that the quadrangle seemed to be full of penguins. He nudged Mildew, but Mildew frowned and shook his head, indicating that it might be wise not to mention it.

"Lord Maudlin," said Sponge.

"Yes, my boy?" said Lord Maudlin.

"Why did the stuffed birds in the cabinets have tiny hats?"

Mildew stared at Sponge, signaling with his eyebrows that asking the famously eccentric Lord Maudlin such a question might not have been the best idea, and this seemed to be justified when Lord Maudlin stopped mid-step and stared at Sponge as though he had never seen him before.

"Well, my boy," said Lord Maudlin eventually, "I tried to put them on living birds, but they simply wouldn't stay on. Not even with the tightest of ribbons, you see."

Sponge opened his mouth with the clear intention of continuing this line of inquiry when Mildew gave his friend a friendly kick in the ankle.

"Ow!" said Sponge.

"I really think we ought to be on our way," said Mildew.

"You don't mean to say you intend to leave without a gift?" said Lord Maudlin.

Mildew and Sponge smiled.

"Of course not, sir," said Mildew. "We'd be delighted."

The boys smiled in anticipation. Lord Maudlin also smiled in anticipation. The anticipation faded on both sides to be replaced by confusion.

"Well?" said Lord Maudlin. "Where's my gift?"

"Oh," said Sponge. "We thought…That is…I'm not sure we have anything for you…"

"Nothing for me?" said Lord Maudlin in astonishment. "Nothing for me?"

Mildew saw the look of panic on Forecourt's face, but what could they possibly give him? Then Sponge reached into Mildew's pocket and waved the Spoon in the air.

"What's that?" said Lord Maudlin.

"That?" said Mildew, frowning at Sponge. "Oh, that's nothing, sir—it's just the School Spoon."

"The School Spoon?" said Lord Maudlin.

"Yes, sir," said Sponge. "This place becomes a school in the future."

"It does?" he said. "What nonsense. Who would come up with such a ridiculous idea?"

"Well, actually, sir," said Mildew, "it's your idea."

"It is?" he said. "Hmmm. Now that you mention it, maybe it is. I do have ideas, you know. Lots of 'em."

Lord Maudlin put the Spoon in his pocket.

"Sir?" said Mildew, holding out his hand. "The Spoon?"

"What?" he said. "A fellow can't give a fellow a gift and then take it back. The very idea! Where did you go to school?"

"But—"

"We'll say no more about it, shall we?" said Lord Maudlin. "Good."

Mildew shook his head and looked up to see Forecourt doing the same.

"Now, come on," said Lord Maudlin with a raise of his eyebrow. "Who are you really?"

Mildew and Sponge looked at each other and sighed.

"Well," said Sponge. "This is my good friend Arthur Wellesley, the first Duke of Wellington, and I am, of course, King George III."

Forecourt raised an eyebrow but said nothing.

"I knew it!" said Lord Maudlin. "Did you hear that, Forecourt?"

"I did, sir," he said with a sigh.

"Now, come on," he said to the poor beleaguered manservant. "There's much to do if Maudlin Towers is to become a school! We must make this a place for the very best and brightest of boys."

Mildew and Sponge exchanged a guilty glance.

"Indeed, sir," said Forecourt.

The boys stood for a few moments as the two men walked off, then made their way toward the bothy and the time machine.

25
The Spoon Reappears

S ponge and Mildew squeezed uncomfortably out of the time machine chair once more and stood rubbing their hips.

"I'm confused, Mildew," said Sponge. "Where—or when—exactly are we now?"

"We should hopefully have arrived in the present but a bit before we left. If my calculations are correct we should have arrived shortly after I arrived back from the Viking village to return the Spoon. It was then I saw Kenningworth on my way to the library to meet you. He was looking shifty in the environs of the trophy room."

"So you suspect Kenningworth after all?" said Sponge. "I thought you said he was too odious to be the culprit."

"Are you sure I said that?"

"Quite sure."

Mildew waved Sponge's objection away.

"I say a lot of things, Sponge. I can't be expected to remember them all."

The two boys peered out from the bothy and, seeing no one about, scrambled down the banks of the ha-ha and set off for the school.

"Quick—to the trophy room!"

The two friends scampered off as fast as their feeble legs would take them, arriving just in time to see Kenningworth sneaking out of the trophy room, Spoon in hand. They saw him put the Spoon in his jacket pocket and walk on.

"Look," whispered Mildew. "It's me."

The two boys peered round a column as the other Mildew and Kenningworth had a brief exchange before the other Mildew headed off to the library to meet the other Sponge.

"We must tell the Headmaster at once!" whispered Sponge.

"No," said Mildew. "The boys will look down on us if we tell. We must confront him and force him to confess ourselves. Come on, Sponge! Let's follow him!"

"But wait," said Sponge. "Doesn't this mean that there are two sets of us in the school at once? That can't be right, Mildew."

"Don't worry, old sock," said Mildew. "The other two of us will have all the adventures we ourselves have just had. Because they are ourselves. So as long as we keep out of their way, they will head off to the bothy, go back and forth in time, and end up being us. Do you see?"

"I suppose so," said Sponge.

He wasn't at all sure he did see, but he hoped by

saying he did the pain in his head might stop. It was a technique he employed regularly in math lessons.

Mildew and Sponge followed Kenningworth at a safe distance until they saw him enter the dorm and close the door behind him.

"Thief!" cried Mildew as he and Sponge burst into the room.

"What are you two doing here?" said Kenningworth, dropping the Spoon in surprise.

"What are you doing, more like?" said Mildew.

"Spoon thief!" cried Sponge.

Kenningworth sighed and sat on his bed. "All right, all right," he said. "Well done. You've caught me. What now?"

They had never seen Kenningworth look so despondent. Or despondent at all, in fact.

"But why?" said Mildew. "Why steal the Spoon when you know its theft will mean the Christmas holidays will be canceled?"

"I wasn't going to steal the Spoon," said Kenningworth. "I didn't even know it was there. It was supposed to be stolen already. I couldn't believe it when I saw it. I had to steal it again."

"But why?" said Mildew.

"Because I was glad the Christmas holidays were canceled!"

The two boys stared at him in astonishment. They had never liked him, but neither would ever have believed he could be so heartless.

"Why?" said Sponge.

Kenningworth took a deep breath.

"Because my Christmas plans had already been canceled, that's why. I was going to be spending Christmas at Maudlin Towers anyway."

"What on earth for?" asked Mildew. "Have you gone mad?"

"Not me. It was Mr. Particle that went mad. I saw him go into that bothy at the edge of the sports field on the last day before the fall holidays. He was looking very shifty and I thought I'd follow him.

"As I was approaching, there was a bright flash from inside and when I opened the door there was no one there. No one at all. I know it sounds unbelievable, but it's true, I swear."

"Go on," said Mildew.

"I was confused, obviously, and left the bothy, closing the door behind me. No sooner had I done so than there was another flash and old Particle appeared at the door and demanded to know what I saw. I asked him how he'd managed to disappear and he mumbled something about explaining it all to me later, then went and told the Headmaster I'd cheated on my test! My father refused to believe me and said I'd have to stay at Maudlin Towers over Christmas as punishment."

"And you thought that if your Christmas was going to be ruined," said Sponge, "you might as well ruin everyone else's. You monster, Kenningworth!"

"Calm yourself, Sponge," said Mildew. "He's not worth it."

"But it makes my soup boil, Mildew!"

"He means blood," said Mildew, catching his friend as he swooned sideways.

"I'm all right," said Sponge dozily. "I'm all right."

"I didn't steal the Spoon the first time!" said

Kenningworth. "The Headmaster canceled Christmas because of that theft, not mine. They were the real monsters in all this, whoever they were."

The boys exchanged another quick glance.

"I don't think we should get bogged down in who is to blame," said Mildew.

"Look," said Kenningworth. "The truth is, I thought that if I had to stay in this hellish place, then at least if I had you boys here with me, it might…it might not be quite so bad. Now I've been caught stealing the Spoon and no one will believe I didn't take it the first time round. I've just made everything a hundred times worse. The boys will think me an absolute fungus. I've been such a fool…"

Kenningworth looked away, and though they could never have dreamed it possible, Mildew and Sponge felt an unexpected onrush of sympathy for their enemy.

"Look," said Mildew after a moment. "Why don't you put the Spoon back? We are the only ones who know, and we shan't tell a soul, will we, Sponge?"

"Of course not," said Sponge.

"Really?" said Kenningworth. "You'd do that for me?"

"Yes," said Mildew. "No one needs to know."

Kenningworth's eyes brimmed with tears.

"Thank you. I shan't forget this."

"Neither shall I," said the Headmaster, appearing from nowhere.

"Sir," said Mildew. "Kenningworth has found the School Spoon. It was stolen again and he—"

"Calm yourself, Mildew," said the Headmaster. "Your attempts to defend Kenningworth are commendable but quite unnecessary. I heard the entire conversation. It seems you have been the victim of an injustice, Kenningworth. Mr. Particle was clearly not himself before he so tragically left us."

"Or *when* he left us, sir," said Mildew.

"Quite," said the Headmaster, casting a suspicious glance in Mildew's direction. "I shall write to your father, Kenningworth, and inform him of Mr. Particle's error."

"It wasn't an error, sir," said Kenningworth. "He knew what he was doing. I've a good mind to—"

"Or," continued the Headmaster with a smile, "I could write to him and inform him you were planning to steal the School Spoon in order to cause the cancellation of the whole school's Christmas holidays."

"Yes, sir," said Kenningworth. "No, sir. Thank you, sir."

"This does not mean that I am not very disappointed in you, Kenningworth. Your father would expect you to set an example to other boys. He was Head Boy at Maudlin Towers, of course."

"Yes, sir," said Kenningworth with a sigh. "I know, sir."

"The important thing here is that the School Spoon has been returned. Quite how that happened or who took it in the first place will, it seems, have to remain a mystery."

Again he cast a suspicious glance at Mildew.

"I think we should all move on and put this unpleasantness behind us," he said.

"Thank you, sir," said Kenningworth.

"Thank you, sir," said Mildew and Sponge.

"You're welcome," said the Headmaster.

The Headmaster beamed and nodded and set off toward his office, Spoon in hand.

An awkward silence followed his departure. Mildew and Sponge looked at Kenningworth. Kenningworth looked at his shoes. Kenningworth looked at Mildew and Sponge. Mildew and Sponge looked at their shoes.

In the end, a small nod seemed to say all that could be said, and they went their separate ways.

Mr. Luckless Sees Reason

The School Spoon had been returned to its natural place and Christmas had been saved. Mildew and Sponge were feeling rather pleased with themselves until they heard a commotion and went to investigate.

They were astonished to see a heated argument and shoving match going on between several of the teachers, with Mr. Luckless at its heart.

"What on earth is going on?" asked Mildew as he stood alongside Enderpenny.

"The teachers appear to have gone mad for Miss Livia," he replied. "Mr. Luckless most of all. It appears that Mr. Drumlin and Mr. Painly have both written poems to her and made the mistake of arriving at the same time to read them aloud. A fight broke out between them and then old Luckless took them both on. Even Stupendo is besotted! Look…"

The boys followed Enderpenny's gaze and, sure enough, there was Mr. Stupendo, heading toward Miss Livia with a small bunch of flowers.

Luckily for all concerned, Big Brian rang for lunch—and there is nothing more important to a teacher than food—so with a few last shoves and mutterings, the teachers headed off to the dining hall, leaving Mr. Luckless standing red-faced and disheveled and Miss Livia looking less than impressed.

"I'd better talk to the Headmaster about Miss Livia and the attic and so on," said Enderpenny. "There's something funny about this whole business."

And before they could stop him, Enderpenny went off in search of the Headmaster.

"Come on, Sponge," said Mildew. "Mr. Luckless needs to be saved from himself."

The boys hurried across the lawn.

"Sir," said Mildew to Mr. Luckless. "You simply must take Miss Livia back to her own time. She's driving the whole school to distraction. It's only a matter of time before someone gets hurt."

"I know you're right," bleated Mr. Luckless forlornly. "But I'm weak. Love is a powerful thing, boys. It's big. Like an elephant. But also soft. Like a … duck."

Mildew and Sponge rolled their eyes.

"You must try and pull yourself together, sir," said Mildew. "Think of the impression you're giving to impressionable types like Sponge here."

Mr. Luckless nodded, his upper lip stiffening beneath his mustache.

"You're right, of course, Mildew."

Just then Mr. Luckless spied Mr. Stupendo talking to Miss Livia, and, scowling, he marched off angrily in that direction, hampered only by Mildew and Sponge hanging on to his gown.

"Sir!" said Mildew. "Stop. Enderpenny is already looking for the Headmaster to tell him about seeing Miss Livia in the attic."

Mr. Luckless stopped in his tracks. "Then I must take Livia back to her own time," he said with a sigh. "She can't stay here. It will never work. I see that. I've been a fool."

"I think it's for the best, sir," said Sponge.

Mr. Luckless took a deep breath and set off toward Mr. Stupendo. After a muttered conversation, Mr. Stupendo wandered off and Mr. Luckless turned his attention to Miss Livia.

The boys could not hear the content of Mr. Luckless's speech, but after a few moments Miss Livia strode toward Mildew and Sponge, waving and frowning, demanding in broken English that

Mr. Luckless take her home "NOW." Her demeanor was quite terrifying—until she saw Sponge.

"Spudge!" cried Miss Livia and swept Sponge up in her arms, showering him with kisses.

Mr. Luckless scowled furiously at Sponge when Miss Livia deposited him back on the ground, his collar and hair awry. Mildew saw the telltale signs of Mr. Luckless working himself up to challenge poor Sponge to a duel, and stepped in briskly.

"Sir," he said. "I really think we must be getting on. Before anyone sees us."

Still glaring warily at Sponge, Mr. Luckless reluctantly agreed. Mildew frowned at the blushing Sponge and shook his head. The quicker things returned to normal, the better for all concerned.

They entered the bothy, and Mr. Luckless sat down in the time machine. Livia turned to each boy in turn, hugging them and kissing them on the forehead.

"Livia," said Mr. Luckless sternly.

Livia rolled her eyes and sat on Mr. Luckless's lap and he pulled the lever, disappearing in a bright flash. A minute or two later he reappeared with a black eye and his clothes askew.

"How did it go, sir?" said Mildew.

"Well, it turns out that Livia neglected to tell me she has a husband in the Roman army stationed in Gaul."

"Oh, sir," said Sponge. "Was he frightfully angry?"

Mr. Luckless massaged his nose.

"He was a tad miffed," he replied. "I thought it best to make a swift exit before someone got hurt."

"Not quite swift enough," said Mildew, pointing to his black eye.

"Agreed," said Mr. Luckless.

Fossilized

"Sir," said Sponge. "The time machine is too dangerous. You must destroy it."

"What?" Mr. Luckless said. "But it's a marvel—perhaps the greatest invention of the age."

"But it's not right, sir," said Mildew. "We weren't meant to travel back and forth in time like cuckoos. It's boggling, sir. The mind wasn't meant to be boggled in that way."

"But it made me interesting," said Mr. Luckless sadly. "I can't give that up."

"You must, sir," said Sponge. "For the greater good."

"The greater good?"

"Yes, sir," said Mildew. "Sponge is right. What would happen if a machine like this got into the hands of someone like Mr. Stupendo? Imagine what havoc he might wreak."

Mr. Luckless nodded, frowning.

"Or the boys, sir," said Sponge. "Imagine if two of the more adventurous boys got their hands on it."

"You're right," he said. "If I keep it, the temptation to return to the past will be too great. It will only be a matter of time before some other lovely lady from the past falls for my charms. I will show you what to do to send it on a one-way journey."

"Show us, sir?" said Mildew. "Why will you not destroy it yourself?"

"I can't bring myself to do it," said Luckless. "I fear I will weaken at the last moment and not go through with it. You boys must provide the strength I do not possess."

"We shall do our best, sir," said Sponge.

Mr. Luckless talked them through the procedure, showing them how to disable the mechanism by removing one of the levers, ensuring that when the machine was sent through time, there would be no means of using it.

"I suggest you send it into the past," said Mr. Luckless. "Into the distant past, where anyone who finds it will not have the technology to repair it and will have no idea what it's for."

The boys nodded. Mr. Luckless left them alone and strode off toward the school, his head hanging forlornly, his gown limp.

"So," said Mildew. "I suppose we'd better get this over with and—"

"What do we have here?" said a voice they both knew and feared. It was Mr. Stupendo, and he was pointing to the time machine.

"Nothing, sir," said Sponge.

"Don't be ridiculous, Sponge," said Mr. Stupendo. "How can it be nothing? It's right there!"

"Where?" said Mildew, looking round in a pretense of not seeing it.

"That!" he yelled, pointing furiously at the time machine. "What is that?"

"It's a—"

"Don't tell him, Mildew!" shouted Sponge.

"Don't tell him what?" said Mr. Stupendo, grabbing Sponge by the lapels and hoisting him into the air until they were eyebrow to eyebrow.

"It's…it's…it's a time machine, sir!" said Sponge.

"What happened to don't tell him?" said Mildew angrily.

"A time machine?" said Mr. Stupendo, dropping Sponge to the floor like a sack of kittens. "What nonsense is this?"

"I'm afraid it's true, sir," said Mildew. "It's a machine for—"

"It's a machine for regaining one's youth, sir," said Sponge.

"No, it's not," said Mildew. "It's a—"

"Shut up, Mildew," said Mr. Stupendo. "What's that you were saying, boy?"

"It's a machine for regaining one's youth, sir," said Sponge. "Or so we were told, sir. It's useless to us, of course. We are still in our youth. It's set to take ten years off one's life, sir, so a little pointless. Although..."

"Yes?"

"Well, might you be interested, sir?"

"Ten years, you say?"

"Yes, sir," said Mildew, slowly realizing what Sponge was up to.

"How does the contraption work, exactly?"

"All you need to do, sir," said Sponge, "is sit down in the chair."

Mildew rearranged the hands of the clock as Mr. Luckless had instructed.

"Yes?" said Mr. Stupendo eagerly, plopping himself down.

"We just have to remove this lever," said Sponge, following Mr. Luckless's instructions.

"And then pull this one," said Mildew.

"This one?"

"Yes, sir."

There was the usual flash and whine, and the chair and its mustachioed occupant were gone. Sponge gasped and almost fainted with the effort involved in his uncharacteristically quick thinking.

"Have we done a terrible thing?" said Sponge after a moment of semi-swooning.

"What? No, no—not at all. Old Stupido will have a whale of a time back in the Stone Age. Perfect time for him. Think of all that running after, and away from, various forms of wildlife, Sponge. He'll be in his element. He's probably making friends with a mammoth as we speak. We've done him a favor."

"I say, Mildew," said Sponge as they started to walk away from the bothy. "Look at this."

Sponge pointed down to a large stone.

"Do you see? I've never noticed it before."

"Yes," said Mildew, looking at the distinct shape of a jaw brimming with teeth set into the rock.

"My father told me all about these," said Sponge. "This is a fossil of an extinct creature that lived in these parts long ago. Longer ago even than the cavemen and such. Dinosaurs, they're called."

"But what's that in its mouth?" said Mildew.

The boys peered closer.

"It appears to be a cog of some kind," said Sponge.

They looked at each other.

"I think we may have sent the time machine a little further back than intended," said Mildew.

"Indeed…So Mr. Stupendo…"

"Don't upset yourself, Sponge," said Mildew. "It wasn't your fault."

"I never said it was," said Sponge.

"Well, it was your idea to tell him that it was a machine to recapture the old goat's lost youth. So in a way…"

"Oh my—you're right," said Sponge. "I sent him to his doom."

"Don't think of it as doom, Sponge," said Mildew. "Think of it as being in a better place."

"How do we know it's a better place?" said Sponge.

"I wasn't meaning for him," said Mildew. "He's in a better place for us. A far, far better place."

Sponge nodded.

"Yes," he said. "When you put it like that."

With that, the boys strolled back toward the school.

"So we really have resolved everything, haven't we?" said Sponge.

"Well, not quite everything, Sponge," said Mildew. "We are still entered in the Hill-Running Tournament."

"Yes, but the only person who knows that is now dodging dinosaurs."

Mildew smiled.

"Good point, Sponge."

"We've sent Miss Livia back to Roman times, we've gotten rid of the time machine and Mr. Stupendo, and we've solved the theft of the School Spoon and the mystery of the two ghosts. I think that's everything."

"Ah, Mildew," said the Headmaster, creeping up

beside them. "Did I hear you mention Miss Livia? Have you seen her? I was hoping to have a word."

"I'm afraid she's gone, sir," said Mildew.

"Gone?"

"Yes, sir," said Mildew. "She is very superstitious apparently and had heard something about the school being haunted."

"Haunted?" said the Headmaster. "Well, how odd. Enderpenny was just telling me that...Oh, never mind. We shall have to make arrangements for a new Latin teacher, I suppose—as well as a new physics teacher, of course..."

There was an awkward silence for a moment or two.

"What about Mr. Luckless for Latin, sir?" suggested Sponge. "I expect he knows quite a lot."

The Headmaster nodded.

"Yes," he said. "Good idea, Spongely-Partwork."

He turned to Mildew with a toothy smile.

"How's that article getting on?"

"Article, sir?"

"Yes—the one about the life of the school. I've told all the teachers and they are, every one of them, fascinated to read it, as will all the boys be, I'm sure."

"Yes, sir," said Mildew.

"Jolly good. Shall we say next week?"

"Well, I—"

"Excellent," said the Headmaster.

He started to walk away, and Mildew groaned.

"Oh," said the Headmaster, turning round and making the boys start. "And I am very much looking forward to the play, Mildew."

"The play? Of course you are, sir."

The Headmaster carried on walking away, humming to himself.

"Sir!" called Sponge.

"Yes?" said the Headmaster.

"We haven't told you about the best part of the article, sir."

"And what is that, Master Spongely-Partwork?"

"It's the section about Mr. Particle, sir," said Sponge. "About his untimely death and whatnot."

"Oh, I don't think we should—"

"But, sir, it's the most fascinating part of the story of the school," said Sponge. "We haven't finished our investigations but there seems to be some connection between Mr. Particle and that awful business with the sheep."

The Headmaster stared at them for a few moments before smiling and tapping his fingertips together.

"You are so very busy with your schoolwork, boys," he said. "I think you should forget all about the article. Just concentrate on the play."

"About that, sir," said Mildew. "We rather thought we might invite the parents to come along to the performance."

"The parents?" said the Headmaster, one eyebrow twitching.

"It will give us a chance to tell them all about the recent excitement regarding the School Spoon and such."

"Perhaps we ought to forget about the play as well," said the Headmaster. "I think we should all try to get back to normal."

"If you're sure?" said Mildew.

"Quite sure," said the Headmaster.

"The boys will be very disappointed," said Mildew.

"Ah well," said the Headmaster. "Please give them my apologies."

The Headmaster walked away, and Mildew patted his friend on the shoulder.

"That was quick thinking, Sponge. Shall we go for lunch?"

"Why not?" said Sponge. "I am quite peckish."

"Me too."

The two boys headed off to the dining hall.

"I won't miss time travel," said Mildew.

"Me neither," agreed Sponge. "Although I suppose we *do* time travel, don't we? Just very slowly and only in the one direction."

"You are a philosopher, Sponge."

"I am?" said Sponge.

"Undoubtedly," said Mildew.

"I rather enjoyed being a detective though."

"Yes—it did have its moments, didn't it?"

"Do you think we'll ever detect again, Mildew?"

"If the school needs us, Sponge. If the school needs us."

And with this thought weighing heavily on their young shoulders, the boys walked on.

Maudlin Towers
Near Lower Maudlin
Cumberland
England

Dear Parents,

Much has happened at the school
but as our esteemed Headmaster
reads all our mail. I will have
to be careful and just say
that ~~████~~ Sponge ~~████~~
~~████████████████████~~
~~████~~ Sponge ~~████~~ Latin
~~████~~ bothy ~~████~~
~~████~~ Christmas ~~████~~
~~████~~ Sponge ~~████~~
~~████████~~ Sponge
!!!!

Just a hint, but rather
exciting, I'm sure you'll agree!

Fondest regards,

Arthur Mildew Esq.

x x x

PS Please send more cookies

Maudlin Towers
Near Lower Maudlin
Cumberland
England

Dear Aunt Bernard,
Thank you for the bed socks
and the very tasty ~~this~~ trifle.
It was a lovely thought, but
perhaps next time put them
in different envelopes. The
letter box at Maudlin Towers is
surprisingly ~~small~~ small.

Many things have occurred.
I will tell you all about
them when I see you at
Christmas.

Your loving nephew,

Algernon
x x x

Ps Mildew says hello

hello!

PPS Please send more cookies

THE AUTHOR

About the Author

Chris Priestley was born and grew old. He has lived in various places for varying amounts of time. He enjoys eating toast and looking at things. Despite all attempts to stop him, he has written and illustrated this book himself. The relevant authorities have been alerted.